JESSICA BECK

THE DONUT MYSTERIES, BOOK 45

DUSTED DISCOVERIES

Donut Mystery 45 DUSTED DISCOVERIES

First edition: 2020

The First Time Ever Published!
DUSTED DISCOVERIES
The 45th Donut Mystery

Jessica Beck is the *New York Times* Bestselling Author of the Donut Mysteries, the Cast Iron Cooking Mysteries, the Classic Diner Mysteries, the Ghost Cat Cozy Mysteries, and more.

WHEN FORMER CHIEF OF Police Phillip Martin finds a clue to a missing treasure while researching a cold case, he, Momma, Jake, and Suzanne go off in search of a valuable relic missing since the Civil War. The only problem is that they aren't the *only* ones looking for the prize, and when word gets out that they are on the hunt as well, things turn ugly, and fast!

This one's for you, dear reader, for taking the journey along with me.
Thank you for being there every step of the way!
And of course, as always,
P and E.

Prologue

"JAKE," I WHISPERED as my foot slipped yet again in the freshly fallen snow and I almost took another tumble down the side of the steep mountain. "Did we lose them?"

My husband shook his head, and then he answered in an even softer voice than I'd used, "No, as far as I can tell, they're still behind us."

"What are we going to do?" I asked as I crept farther along the trail, being as quiet as I could manage. It had started to snow in earnest just after we'd left my Jeep, and the trail was now slick from the accumulation. Not only that, but every time I brushed up against a tree branch or a tall weed, I got covered with wet snow again. To make matters even worse, the temperature had been steadily falling ever since we'd gotten onto the trail, and I dreaded the thought of how cold it might be that night if we didn't make it back to my Jeep in time.

"What can we do? We keep moving," he said, the resolution thick in his voice.

I suddenly realized that worrying about the night was a different problem, so far down the line that I could barely let it concern me.

First we had to escape the man stalking us on the trail, intent on killing us.

It was still hard for me to believe that what had started off as a lark, an exciting quest with three people I loved very much, had so quickly turned into a cat-and-mouse game of life and death.

And at that moment, I felt very much like someone else's prey.

Chapter 1
The Day Before

"SUZANNE, HOW WOULD you like to be rich?" my stepfather and the one-time police chief of April Springs, North Carolina, Phillip Martin, asked me as I wiped the counter at Donut Hearts, my donut shop nestled in the heart of town. My assistant, Emma Blake, had left the shop early, citing a class at the nearby college, but I had a hunch she'd just wanted to squeeze in some time with her boyfriend, the amazing chef Barton Gleason. It had been easy enough letting her go. After all, we had been having one of our slow days at the donut shop, and I'd been by myself for the past twenty minutes, debating whether I should stick around or just shut the place down early and see what my husband, Jake, was up to.

"Oh, I don't know," I said as I continued to work. "I'm pretty sure that being that wealthy isn't everything it's cracked up to be, what with taxes and people constantly asking you for money," I added as I finished that chore and started collecting plates and coffee cups from a few of the nearby empty tables.

"Suzanne, I'm serious," he said. "I'm talking about the real deal here."

I looked at Phillip for a moment, studying the older man who had once been portly. He had lost a great deal of weight in order to woo my mother, and he had been fighting to keep the pounds off ever since he'd won her heart.

"What are you talking about?" I asked as I kept working.

"I'm talking about the Southern Shooting Star," he said with hushed breath. Even though we were the only two people in Donut Hearts at the moment, he still looked around to be certain that no one was listening. "I've found it."

"Really? Cool! Let's see it," I said, suddenly interested. The Star, as it had been known by one and all in the South since the Civil War, had been cast out of a great deal of Confederate gold and then encrusted with rubies and emeralds from some of the wealthiest families below the Mason Dixon line. Unfortunately, it hadn't been sold to the highest bidder in time to do the Confederacy any good, and the priceless artifact had been shuffled from private collection to private collection over the years, only being displayed four times in the first hundred years after the war had ended. Then, in 1965, it had been stolen from a museum exhibit in Charlotte, and no one had seen it since.

"I don't actually have it on me," Phillip explained. "It's pretty heavy."

"Is it at your place with Momma, then?" I asked. "I can shut down early and go with you to take a look at it, since I seem to be completely out of clientele at the moment, anyway."

"I said that I've found it, not that I have it. As a matter of fact, the Star isn't in April Springs," he corrected me.

"Is it at least in North Carolina?"

"No, but it's just over the Virginia border. I need to put a team together to retrieve it, and I naturally thought of you and Jake. What do you say? Are you interested in an equal share of the reward for finding a national treasure?"

"What would I do about the donut shop while I was gone?" I asked as I looked around. "I can't leave it to Emma and Sharon for more than a few days."

"Honestly, it shouldn't take much longer than that," Phillip said. "Unless I'm mistaken, we'll be there and back in less time than that."

"What did Jake say when you asked him?" I asked Phillip as I switched the OPEN sign on the door to CLOSED.

"I haven't asked him yet," my stepfather answered. "I thought I should come to you first."

"Really? I figured he'd be your *first* stop," I said as I got further into my closing routine.

"I know *he* won't take any convincing," Phillip said, and I realized that my stepfather was probably right. Jake had recently taken on some freelance consulting jobs with police forces in the vicinity, but lately there had been a shortage of cases coming his way. "I knew from the start that you were going to be the hardest one to sell on the idea."

"Do you mean my mother is already on board?" I asked him skeptically.

"When I told her about it, she said that it sounded like it might be fun," he said with a grin. "You should have seen how excited she was when I told her about it."

I looked at him carefully. "Hang on a second. There's not a *map* leading to it, is there? Does X mark the spot, by any chance?"

"Joke if you want, but this is serious. There's no map. I found something that mentioned the Star buried in the personal papers of Tommy Gun Malone. The last rumor I could track down about the Star was that Malone had stolen it just before he'd been arrested for killing Mad Dog Magee. The code was hidden within a letter to Tommy's sister, but the meaning was clear enough, once I figured out what it meant."

"I've got a question for you," I asked.

"Go ahead and shoot. I'll answer it if I can."

"Why do so many bad guys have such colorful names?" I asked him as I started sweeping the floor. "Tommy Gun Malone. Mad Dog Magee. Why aren't any of them just named Fred?"

"Is that *really* the question that's most on your mind?" Phillip asked, clearly getting a little frustrated by my lack of enthusiasm.

"Sorry. How did the letter happen to end up with you?"

He grinned. "I traced his personal correspondence and other papers back to his last living heir, and after I had those in my hands, I found the hint, more of a reference really, in a letter he wrote to his sister from prison."

"And she just handed it over to you?" I asked as I began to empty the display cases of our unsold donuts for the day. There were seventeen left, nine of them my new butterscotch toffee cake donuts. I had enjoyed them, but clearly my customers hadn't, and they'd have to go back to the drawing board before I was willing to offer them for sale again. The donut world was like that sometimes. What I thought would be a surefire hit was sometimes a flop, and what I barely cared enough to put out for sale seemed to do amazingly well.

"That's the thing. She died before she even received it. It ended up as a part of her estate, which was basically just a cardboard box full of mail, old bills, and recipes. I bought the lot off of her grandson, a kid named Henry, and then I started carefully going through it. Another collector was all set to buy it, but I swooped in with more cold hard cash at the last second, and I got it instead. That's when I found the letter."

"What did the box cost you?" I asked him.

"It doesn't matter," he said abruptly.

"Phillip."

"I gave him a hundred dollars for it," he said, but before I could protest, he quickly added, "but I had no idea that reference was even in there. I was trying to solve another cold case I'm sure Tommy committed, and I was looking for a reference to that, not the Star. Don't worry about Henry. I'll see to it that he gets a nice reward, once we've collected our take from the insurance company."

"Wow, you're really sure we'll find it, aren't you?"

"I'm dead certain of it," he said.

I'd never liked that expression. It reminded me too much of what other people had lost. In the course of my life of investigating murder as an amateur sleuth, I'd seen more than enough dead bodies to last me a lifetime.

I thought about it for a full moment, and then I nodded. "Okay, if Jake's in, then I am, too."

"Excellent. We leave tomorrow morning at sunrise," he said with a grin. "Suzanne, this is going to be a blast."

"I hope you're right," I replied as I started the cash register report and began totaling our cash on hand to make sure that they matched the shop for the day. It just so happened that my assistant, Emma, and her mother, Sharon, were already set to take over Donut Hearts for the next two days anyway, so if that was really all the time that it would take, I didn't even have to clear it with anyone first.

It appeared that I was about to go on a treasure hunt with my husband, my mother, and my stepfather.

What could possibly go wrong?

Chapter 2

"I STILL THINK MY NEW truck would have been fine for this trip," Jake said in the passenger seat beside me as I drove my Jeep the next day deeper and deeper into the mountains, heading for Virginia. We had been getting light freezing rain all morning, though it was still warm enough to keep the roads free, but not by a lot, and I was glad I had all-weather tires on my vehicle.

"I'd hardly call it new."

"Okay then, it's new to me, so it feels new."

I smiled over at him. "Jake, your truck hasn't been new since the middle of the last century. It's not built for the kind of weather we're already facing. I still can't believe Phillip talked us into this with the weather forecast we're looking at."

"I think it could be fun," my husband said. "Besides, Phillip got to bring *his* truck," he added a bit sullenly.

I had to laugh. What was it about boys and their toys? "I promise you that you can drive us anywhere you'd like, as long as it's at least eighty degrees out," I said. "Don't forget, Phillip's truck has four-wheel drive. You said yourself that it could climb the side of a tree if it had to."

"Don't forget, *I* have two trucks," Jake said softly, and then he grinned. "Though I admit neither one is particularly suited for this weather." He looked out the windshield and watched some of the ice accumulate on the wipers. "Should we stop so I can clear them?"

"No, it's all right," I said, though in truth the icy streaks did make visibility a little tougher than normal. "We're almost there, aren't we?"

He looked at the folding paper map in his lap. My husband didn't believe in GPS. He was old school, and he loved the elegant older technology. "The Virginia State Line should be right around the next bend, and Devil's Ridge should be approximately five miles after that."

"That's not too bad, then," I said, focusing on the winding road that kept going up.

"It might just be five miles, but it's another thousand feet in elevation," Jake said as he gestured out the window. "This could all be snow once we get there."

I didn't relish the prospect of tromping around in that. I wasn't a fan of being cold, or wet, for that matter. Being both made me very unhappy. "I thought the forecast said it was going to clear up though, didn't it?"

"Forecasts have been known to be wrong," Jake said with a shrug.

"So have vague references to buried treasure," I added. "Do you honestly think the Southern Shooting Star is where Phillip believes it is?"

"Nobody said it was buried, but I looked over the documents last night after we agreed to go," Jake said. "I'm guessing that unless someone else has already stumbled across the Star by accident, it's going to be right where the letter says it is. It would be too much of a coincidence for someone to just stumble onto it randomly."

"Funny, but I never took you for a treasure hunter," I told my husband with a smile, risking a quick look in his direction.

"There's more pirate in me than I care to admit," he said with a hint of laughter. There was no doubt that Jake's mood had improved dramatically since he'd started doing consulting work with different police forces, and that was something I was very happy about. "Suzanne, this has the potential to be huge."

"Are you going to be crushed if we don't find it?"

"The truth is, I'm excited about the adventure of it," Jake admitted. "It would be great to find the Star, but I'm not counting on it, at least not like Phillip is."

"What I don't understand is why. It's not as though they need the money the reward for its recovery would bring," I said. "Momma has more than enough for both of them."

"That's the thing, though," Jake said. "This is something *he'd* be providing. I know approximately what his pension is for being a retired chief of police, and it's nowhere near what your mother brings in on a daily basis. It's a matter of pride with him, Suzanne."

"I understand," I said. While Jake had brought a tremendous amount of savings with him into our marriage, he hadn't had a regular source of income for some time. Despite that, he'd still insisted that we split our expenses right down the middle. I had a feeling that pride rang strong through *all* men, but Southern men seemed especially vulnerable to its siren song.

"Good. For his sake, let's hope it's still there, then," Jake said. He kept glancing behind us, which was odd, since Momma and Phillip were in the truck ahead of us.

"Is something wrong?"

"Old habits die hard, I guess," he said. "It's probably just my imagination, but I think that black SUV behind us has been following us for the last forty miles."

I glanced in my rearview mirror and saw a large and shiny vehicle three cars behind us. It was too far away to make out who was driving, and for all I knew, it could have been a family heading off for vacation or a traveling salesman trying to make his rounds. "I'm sure it's nothing."

"Probably," Jake said, but I noticed that his admission didn't stop him from glancing back again from time to time.

I did the same and nearly ran off the icy road as I heard the warning bumps that signaled I'd drifted too far off course.

"Why don't you leave the rear surveillance to me, and you focus on getting us there in one piece," he said with a smile.

"That's probably a good plan," I said. After a few minutes, I added, "I can't believe that in a few hours, we could be holding one of the most sought-after remnants of the Civil War in our hands."

"A great many people have been searching for it since it disappeared in the sixties," Jake said. "In a way, it's almost going to be a shame if we discover where it's been all this time."

"That's certainly one way of looking at it. Sometimes I forget what a romantic spirit you have behind that gruff exterior," I told him.

He brushed my hair off my shoulder. "I'd love to prove to you how romantic I am right here and now, but I really do think you should concentrate on the road."

"I didn't mean that kind of romance, and you know it," I said, swatting his leg and laughing. "I'm talking about the legend versus the reality."

"Well, I like to *think* I'm a legend," he said with a grin. When I didn't respond, he asked, "Is the reality much different from that?"

"Trust me, you're every bit a legend to me," I answered, matching his smile with one of my own.

"There's the turnoff," Jake said suddenly as he gestured to a side road off the main highway. I might have missed it if he hadn't been there to point it out to me.

As I took the sharp turn, I asked, "What happened to the sign pointing us to Devil's Ridge?"

"It must have come down in the last storm," Jake explained. "I might not have seen it myself if Phillip hadn't made the turn." He pivoted in his seat and watched behind us in silence.

"Is it still back there?" I asked him, knowing that he was looking to see if the SUV had followed suit.

"No, it kept going north," Jake said with a shrug. "You're probably right. It was just my imagination after all."

"Old habits die hard, don't they?" I asked sympathetically.

"More than you could possibly know," he replied.

I decided not to ask him what he meant by that. I'd found in the past that sometimes it was better not to ask when I wasn't sure I'd like the answer.

The moment of gloom that had visited us quickly faded away as we came into the small town of Devil's Ridge. From what I could see from the main road, there was a restaurant, a post office, a police station and jail, a small grocery and gas station, and two dozen houses lining the main drag. I could see other offices and buildings shooting off branches on either side of the road. I figured the place was probably half the size of April Springs, making it my kind of town, but unlike my home, a place that felt friendly and warm most of the time, Devil's Ridge seemed to have a more ominous tone to it, as though a dark shadow was hanging over it.

I shivered a bit.

"Are you cold?" Jake asked.

"That's part of it, I guess," I admitted.

"It's a little bit gloomy, isn't it? The mountains are so close on either side of town that not a lot of sunlight gets in, especially in this weather," Jake said. "At least it stopped raining, or sleeting, or whatever that was."

"I'd call it a wintry mix, and yeah, you're right, I'm glad it stopped," I admitted as I followed Phillip down one of the side roads until we came to an old hotel, three stories tall and taking up a fair amount of space. There must have been thirty rooms in the place, and I had to wonder if they'd ever managed to hang up their No Vacancy sign. The white paint was chipped and fading from the wooden clapboards, and the green shutters had peeling paint as well. The weeds around the hotel grounds were in dire need of attention, but I doubted they would get it until spring. On the right side, a steep drop-off loomed, and I wondered why they hadn't put a fence in front of it to keep people from falling off the hillside. A sign above the front door said, THE OVERLOOK INN, and it too was starting to fade.

"Hang on a second. Wasn't the Overlook the name of the hotel in that Stephen King novel?" I asked Jake as we parked.

"It's a pretty common name, I'd imagine," Jake said as he got out, "especially with a view like that," he added as he gestured toward the drop-off.

We got out and met up with Phillip and Momma, saving our bags for later.

"Isn't it magnificent?" Phillip asked as he gazed up at the place.

"Sure, I suppose you could say that," I answered skeptically.

"What's the matter? Don't you like it? Just wait until you see it inside," he answered enthusiastically.

"What can I say? My husband has a fondness for old things," my mother said. All it took was a grin from me for her to know what I was about to say next. "Suzanne, this is a pleasure trip, remember? Let's leave our caustic comments behind, shall we?"

I hugged her, letting the crack about her age die on my lips. "We shall. Thanks again for inviting us."

"Of course," Momma said with a slight smile. "It wouldn't be the same without you."

"Should we grab our bags now or go inside and check in, and then get them later?" Phillip asked impatiently.

Momma smiled at him. "Honestly, I haven't seen you this excited since I agreed to marry you."

"Oh, I think I've been *at least* that excited a few times since," Phillip said with a grin.

It did my heart good to see my mother blush. "Be that as it may, let's go see what the lobby looks like."

"After you," Phillip said with a flourish as he bowed at the waist. Jake shrugged, and then he bowed as well.

Momma and I walked into the inn laughing.

This was going to be fun.

At least that was what I thought at the time.

Chapter 3

"WELCOME TO THE OVERLOOK Inn," a heavyset man in his early thirties said wearily as we approached the front desk. His brass name tag said *Mr. Garrett*. The window to the right showed the overlook the place had undoubtedly been named for. That side of the inn featured a fairly close drop-off into a bit of a precipice. It made for a spectacular view of the mountains, though I knew that it must have been a constant worry to the inn's owner. There was a single sign in the middle of the expanse beyond the trees that said, "Keep To The Path," but that was it. I for one wouldn't want to go stumbling around out there in the dark.

"Is everything okay, Mr. Garrett?" I asked him.

"What? Oh, of course it is. Never better. Forgive me. It's just been a long day."

I glanced at my watch and saw that it was barely past one in the afternoon. "When exactly did today start for you?" I asked him with a grin.

"Yes, it does seem early in the day to be complaining, but my night clerk failed to show up for work last night, so I had to fill in for him myself." After stretching his neck for a moment, he said, "You must be the Martins and the Bishops."

"What gave us away, Mr. Garrett?" Jake asked him.

"I'd like to say that it is my keen sense of my guests, but as a matter of fact, yours are the only new reservations we have for tonight. What can I say? It's the slow season here at the Overlook. We don't have any ski slopes close enough to matter, and the autumn leaves are long gone. Most of the folks we get here this time of year are simply trying to get away from other things. What brings you all to our part of the Virginia corner of the Blue Ridge Mountains?"

"Pleasure," Momma and I said at the same time as Jake and Phillip answered, "Business."

"Actually, it's none of my business. I'm just to be hosting you," he said, though I saw him try to hide his smile.

"As a matter of fact, it's a little bit of both," I told the innkeeper.

"Well, whatever the reason you are all here, I'm glad you could join us. Mr. and Mrs. Martin, you're in room 215, and Mr. and Mrs. Bishop, you'll be in room 213."

I felt my breath flee my chest as he'd announced Momma's room number. If he'd said room 217 to us, I might just run screaming from the hotel. There were just so many coincidences I could take, and 217 had some very bad vibes associated with it in the book and in the movies.

Mr. Garrett must have noticed my response to the room numbers he'd just given us. The innkeeper grinned as he handed us each an old-fashioned key on a large brass fob, nothing like the new credit card keys most places used these days. "Don't worry, Mrs. Bishop, I see that same reaction all of the time," he explained. "I won't use 217 unless it's a dire emergency."

"What exactly is the significance of 217?" Momma asked.

I was about to tell her when Mr. Garrett answered for me. "The Stephen King novel *The Shining* takes place in a hotel/resort in the Colorado Mountains. The hotel is named the Overlook, and some very bad things happen in room 217. The significance of the book and the movies have not been lost on us, trust me. Would you believe that some folks actually *request* that room?"

"That makes them all braver souls than me," I admitted. I remembered reading that book for the first time with all of the lights in the place on and not being able to sleep for hours after I'd finished it anyway. It hadn't helped matters that I'd been living alone in the cottage at the time.

"It takes all kinds," Jake said.

"Would you like help with your bags?" he asked us. "I assume they are still in your car."

"Cars," Jake corrected him.

"Actually, they're driving a Jeep, and we're in my truck," Phillip added.

"Anyway, thanks for the offer, but we can get them ourselves," Jake said.

"Is there a good place to eat lunch around here?" Phillip asked.

I was hungry, too, but I hadn't wanted to be the one to say something first. After all, we were there on a mission to find the Southern Shooting Star, but if Phillip was willing to postpone the recovery in order to eat, then I was absolutely all for it.

"The DINE is one street over, one block down," he told us. "This time of year, we offer breakfast and dinner here at the inn, but no lunch. We do hope you will all join us for dinner this evening."

"I'm sure we will," Momma said, and then she turned to us. "What do you all think? Shall we eat first, see to a little business, and then bring our luggage up to our rooms and have a relaxing afternoon before dinner?"

"That sounds like a great plan to me," I said with a grin. As long as eating was our first priority, I was more than happy to go along with the rest of her proposed schedule.

"Why is it called the DINE?" I asked the woman barely into her twenties who greeted us at the cash register as we walked in. Her rich red hair nearly reached her waist, and she sported the most intricate set of curls I'd ever seen in my life. Her name, if her badge was correct, was Eleanora, and she was the *only* thing in the place under thirty, including the furnishings. There were cracked red vinyl booths throughout the restaurant, tables with scarred linoleum tops, and a faded black-and-white-checked floor covering that had seen better days. Even given the shabby state of the place, it was crowded with diners, and I noticed only two free tables among the eleven eating areas. One taken table in particular was odd. The sign over it said "Reserved for the Liar's Club," and two older men were sitting there sharing the latest local gossip from the sound of it.

"The R fell off seven years ago," Eleanora explained. "After a tornado swept through here and knocked off the R, Billy was too cheap to replace it. Instead, he marked through all of the menus with a Sharpie, and when it came time to print up new ones, he decided to keep up the tradition. We've been the DINE ever since."

"I like it," I said. "It has character."

"If you say so," the young waitress said with a shrug. "We've all just gotten used to it. Feel free to sit wherever you'd like to, as long as nobody else is sitting there at the moment," she added with a grin. "I'll be right with you."

Instead of walking us to one of the free tables, she handed us four one-page menus and turned to ring up a customer's meal.

After we settled into the booth and placed our orders, four specials featuring country-style steak, mashed potatoes, and green beans, I looked at Phillip curiously.

"Why are you looking at me like that, Suzanne?" he asked me when he noticed that I was watching him.

"I just can't believe you were willing to stop for lunch before we went off in search of...you know," I substituted lamely, not wanting to mention the Star by name, just in case anybody around us happened to be listening in.

"I wanted to, but I didn't think it would be fair to the three of you," he admitted. "Besides, I've waited this long. What's another half hour?"

"I admire your restraint," I said as Eleanora came back to freshen our sweet teas, though we'd barely had time to drink much at all. I noticed that she spent a considerable amount of time smiling at Jake, but who could blame her? My husband was a handsome man, even though he always underestimated his appeal to women.

"Don't look now, but I think you've got yourself a fan," I told Jake after she was gone.

"Who? That child? Don't be ridiculous, Suzanne."

"I noticed it, too, Jake," Momma said. "She is rather fetching."

"I suppose she's pretty enough, but *I* prefer shapely brunettes in their thirties over slim redheads barely out of their teens," he said as he squeezed my hand.

"Nice save, pal," I said with a grin.

"I wasn't trying to save anything," he said, matching my smile with one of his own. "What can I say? I'm hopelessly in love with my wife."

"Funny you should say that, because there seems to be a lot of that going around," Phillip said as he reached over and squeezed Momma's hand.

I laughed and then smiled at my mother. "Who knew we'd both end up picking such smooth-talking men?" The irony was that neither man was exactly known for expressing their affection so easily. Maybe it had something to do with the weather or, more likely, our mission.

"I'm not about to complain," Momma answered.

"No, me either," I said.

Eleanora came back with our food, and I saw a slight frown tick across her lips as she put the plates down in front of us. I had a feeling that she wasn't used to being ignored, especially by men, and clearly she didn't like it. Jake's plate in particular seemed to land in front of him with quite a bit more force than was necessary.

"Oh, well. Easy come, easy go," I said as I winked at him after she was gone.

Instead of responding in any way whatsoever, he took a bite of his country-style steak. "Hey, that's really good."

"Don't let Trish or Hilda hear you say that," I cautioned him. The Boxcar Grill's owner and main cook back in April Springs were both very proud of the food they served, and with good reason.

"I wouldn't dream of it," he said.

I took a bite myself and saw that he was right. While it wasn't quite up to the Boxcar's standards, it was close.

We ate our meals, chatting about everything and anything but the Southern Shooting Star, and after we paid our split bills, we walked out, leaving Eleanora a nice tip to make up for her bruised ego.

"Do we need to go back to your truck to get the exact location of the object?" Jake asked Phillip as he rubbed his hands together briskly. The temperature was definitely dropping outside, but at least there wasn't any precipitation.

"No need for that," Phillip said with a grin as he patted his jacket pocket. "These days, I never go anywhere without it."

"Then let's go find ourselves some treasure," I said excitedly.

It was hard to believe that in mere minutes, we'd be recovering one of the most sought-after icons of the Civil War.

Chapter 4

"I DON'T UNDERSTAND. It should be right here," Phillip said with frustration as he felt for a loose set of bricks in the short wall that stood in front of the town's library. From what I could see, every single brick was mortared firmly in place, even the main brick in question.

"Are you sure you read the location correctly?" Jake asked him.

"Seven up, eighteen over from the left lion," he said.

There was a pair of old concrete lions sitting on either corner column of the walkway that led to the library. I counted again myself, and sure enough, Phillip was at the right brick in question.

"Somebody must have already found it and filled the mortar back in," Momma said with a sigh. "I'm sorry, Phillip. I know how important this was to you, but it's been over half a century. Someone else was *bound* to stumble across it."

"Then why haven't we heard anything about the Star being found?" Jake asked.

"Maybe they don't know what they've got," Momma suggested.

"I highly doubt that, but it could be that they don't want anyone else to know that they have it," I added.

"Why would you keep something like that to yourself?" Phillip asked.

"I can think of a handful of reasons," I said.

"Name three," my stepfather insisted.

"One, they're afraid someone might take it, two, they might not be in a position to go public with their find, and three... I don't know."

"They're waiting for the 'right time' to discover it someplace else," Jake supplied.

"I have a fourth reason," Momma said. "Perhaps they are more interested in owning the Star anonymously themselves than just accepting the reward for its recovery."

"I guess it doesn't matter, does it?" Phillip asked. "I was so sure that it would be here. I'm sorry I dragged you all here on a wild goose chase."

"Don't think of it that way," Momma said.

"How should I think of it?" he asked glumly.

"We've had a nice chance to get away. That is in and of itself enough of a reason to be here, at least in my opinion."

As she spoke, Jake touched my arm lightly and pointed toward the road.

Cruising past the library was the same black SUV we'd seen earlier on the road to Devil's Ridge.

Jake took off at a dead run after them, not even stopping to tell Momma and Phillip what he was doing.

"What's going on?" Phillip asked as he took up the chase as well, even though he didn't have a clue about why he was running.

"They followed us here to Devil's Ridge," I told Momma as I took off after them, too.

I wasn't really surprised when my mother failed to follow in pursuit.

When I got out to the main road, Jake and Phillip were standing there looking each way.

Unfortunately, there was no black SUV in sight.

"Any idea where they went?" I asked.

"No, by the time we got up to the main road, they were already gone," Jake said.

"You know, it still might not be anything," I told him.

"I know, but my gut is telling me that it's related to Phillip's treasure."

"I wish it was mine," he said, and then he quickly corrected, "Ours, I mean." He pulled the letter out yet again, studied it offhand, and then took another, more intense, look at the library itself.

"This isn't right," he said flatly.

"We know," I said. "We saw the mortared brick, too."

"No, what I'm saying is that this isn't the right library."

"Phillip, I can only imagine how disappointed you must be, but I refuse to believe that a town this size has more than one library in its city limits."

"He's right," Jake said. "I was so focused on the brick wall that I didn't really pay any attention to the library itself. This building wasn't around fifty years ago. I'd stake my reputation on it."

Phillip walked toward the library and pointed to a cornerstone on the lower left side of the building. "It says 2014."

"That has to mean that the library moved," I said, nodding.

"Which makes me wonder where the old library used to be," Momma said.

"We could always just go in and ask someone," I said, pointing to the main door.

I started off to do just that when Phillip spoke up quickly. "I'd rather not rouse anyone's suspicions if I can help it if it's all the same to you," he said.

"That's all well and good, but I'm not sure how we're going to find the old library without asking someone around here," I told him.

"There are other ways," Momma said.

"Go on. We're listening," Jake said.

"Suzanne, you're always telling me what a boon the Internet is to your investigations. Don't you think there's a good chance we'll find a reference to the old library's location online?"

"Probably, but I'm not sure how good a job I can do tracking it down with just my phone," I admitted.

"My laptop's in the truck," Phillip said. "We can use that."

"You brought it with you?" Momma asked him incredulously.

"I wanted to have it handy, just in case we needed it," he admitted. "Remember, since I retired from being the chief of police, that's how I spend most of my time these days. As a matter of fact, now that I think about it, I'm sure I've got an old map of Devil's Ridge in my files somewhere."

"Are those in the truck as well?" Momma asked.

He looked a bit sheepish as he admitted, "I couldn't stand the thought of leaving them back at the cottage," Phillip said.

"Good for you," Jake said, slapping his back. "Let's head back and take a look."

When we got back to our vehicles though, it was obvious that someone had broken into Phillip's truck.

The passenger-side window had been smashed, and there were shards of glass all over the seat and the floor.

"Is *everything* gone?" Momma asked.

"No, it appears that just about everything is still here," he said as he lifted up the handle and flipped the seat forward. "Strike that. My computer and all of my hard files are missing."

"Now I *know* that black SUV isn't just a coincidence," Jake said.

"Do you honestly think that whoever did this was driving that vehicle?" Momma asked him.

"Think about it. They saw all four of us at the library and rushed straight over here while they knew we were occupied elsewhere. If it was a common theft, they would have taken your bags, too."

"The Jeep's fine," I said as I rejoined them. We'd parked a few spaces away, and the first thing I'd thought of was to check the contents of my car. "The bags are still all there."

"Was it broken into as well?" Momma asked.

"No, but nobody needed to force their way in. The passenger side's door lock has been sticking lately, so I haven't been locking it. I've been meaning to get it looked at, but I never managed to get around to it."

"So someone may or may not have searched our luggage, too," Jake said as he pulled out his overnight bag and zipped it open. After a quick search, he said, "Nobody's been through this."

"How can you be certain?" Momma asked him.

"I've got a very particular way I pack my bags," Jake said. "It's something I picked up over time, and trust me, I'd know if anyone had been rifling through my things."

"What about you, Suzanne?" Phillip asked me.

"I could check, but I'm not entirely certain I'd know if they took some of my stuff, let alone searched the bag. I just jammed some things I thought I might need into it and then tossed it into the Jeep, along with spare shoes for Jake and me."

Momma frowned for a moment, but instead of commenting, she said, "Let's just assume for the sake of argument that they never got to your Jeep. The question becomes, why not?"

"I can think of two reasons," Jake said. "Either they were interrupted while they were breaking into Phillip's truck, or they started there and found what they were looking for, so there was no need to continue their search." He turned to my stepfather. "What all was in those notes of yours?"

"Everything but the letter from Tommy Gun to his sister," Phillip admitted glumly.

"You didn't make a copy of that?" Jake asked him.

"Of course I did," Phillip said as he patted his pocket. "That's what I've been carrying around. The original is back at the cottage. There was no way I was going to risk bringing that with us."

Jake nodded. "Is it hidden well there?"

"Jacob, you don't actually believe that someone would break into our home in April Springs, do you?"

"I wouldn't put it past them," Jake said.

"Who exactly is 'them'? The stranger in the SUV?" Momma asked him.

"Maybe. Probably. I'm not sure yet, but somehow someone got wind of what Phillip was up to, and they decided to claim the Southern Shooting Star for themselves," he said ominously. "No matter what."

"But they haven't attacked us directly," Momma said, clearly disturbed by the prospect.

"No, that's true," Jake said.

I knew there was a second part to his statement that he wasn't verbalizing, but I didn't want it just out there hanging in the air. "At least not yet, you mean," I supplied.

Jake and Phillip both nodded.

"We should call someone," Momma said resolutely.

"You're right. I saw a body shop on the way in," Phillip said. "It's cold, and the weather could turn worse any time. I don't relish driving back down the mountain like this, do you?"

As he got the number on his phone to call, Momma looked at him oddly. "I was talking about someone in law enforcement, Phillip."

"Momma, we have a former police chief and a state police inspector here with us. Who exactly do you think we should call, the Mounties?"

"You're right," my mother said with a quick nod. "I doubt the law enforcement officers in Devil's Ridge are up to the standards of our husbands." She turned to both men and then added, "I apologize, gentlemen."

"No apologies needed," Jake said with a grin. "As a matter of fact, after Phillip makes his call and arranges the window repair, I suggest we go speak with the police chief of Devil's Ridge."

"If you're certain that is the course of action you'd like to take," Momma said, clearly approving of the idea. "Let's *all* go, shall we?"

Jake looked a bit uncomfortable, but to his credit, Phillip was the one who spoke up. "Actually, it should just be Jake and me, Dot. We can present our credentials and have a nice little chat that we can't have if you two are with us. I'm sorry, but that's the way it needs to be." He said the last bit as though it cost him more than I knew, but he was right. I just hoped that Momma could see it.

"Very well," she said. The phrase could have been full of anger and animosity, but instead it was couched in acceptance, which both men accepted gracefully. "What do you propose we do while you're handling that?"

"We can store your bags in the Jeep for now," I told her.

"That depends," Momma said.

"On?" I asked.

"Is your door lock still not functioning properly?"

"Well, I haven't had time to fix it since I told you about it, if that's what you're asking me," I said with a shrug.

"Suzanne, this is no time to be impertinent," she said.

"Sorry, I'll try to be more pertinent, then," I replied. "I'm open to suggestions. What did you have in mind?"

"Why don't we take our bags to our rooms and then decide what we're going to do while the men are off making new friends?"

"Sounds good to me," I said.

"We'll help you carry the bags, Dot," Jake said, clearly uncomfortable with her proposal.

She wasn't having any of that, though. "We are perfectly capable of moving two bags each," she said a bit primly. "You don't doubt that, do you?"

"No, ma'am," he said, quickly cowed by her tone. "Not for one second."

She could see his reaction just as easily as the rest of us could. Taking a step forward, she put a hand lightly on his shoulder and smiled. "As much as my daughter and I appreciate the gesture, we'll be fine. Now make your calls. We'll catch up with you later." She then turned to me and added, "Are you coming, Suzanne?"

"I'm right behind you," I answered. As I headed to the Jeep to get my bag and Jake's, I glanced back at my husband. He offered me a sheepish shrug, and I winked at him. He understood better than most that the Hart women could bite when the occasion warranted it. Momma's rebuke had been the mildest possible, but he'd clearly taken it a bit harder than I'd hoped. I'd have to make sure later to offer him a bit of comfort. After all, no one alive more than me had been on the receiving end of those barbs, most of them much worse than he'd just received.

As I shouldered both our bags, I looked up to see Momma struggling a bit with her burdens, but after her speech to Jake, none of us were going to offer her any help at all. She knew that, too, I was sure, but I was glad when we walked back into the hotel lobby and she could put everything down on a nearby luggage cart.

The joy didn't last, though.

I looked up, expecting to see the manager at least offer us a smile or even a greeting, but he was clearly so troubled by something that he didn't even acknowledge our presence.

Enough was enough.

It was time to get to the bottom of his problems, whether it was any of my business or not.

Chapter 5

"MR. GARRETT, WHAT'S wrong?" I asked the hotel manager. Before he could brush off my question, I added, "There's no use trying to duck the question, because my mother and I aren't leaving the front desk until you tell us."

Momma looked surprised for an instant, but then she nodded in agreement. I loved that she was willing to back me up without any warning. To be fair, I would do the same for her if the occasion ever arose. My entire life she'd always been the steady one, my rock, someone I could always count on. It had driven me crazy as a teen, but that was the funny thing about it. The older I got, the smarter she seemed to get. "Come, sir, it's a reasonable question."

"I only wish that I had a reasonable answer," Garrett said with a sigh.

"That's okay. We'll take an *unreasonable* one," I said with my best reassuring smile.

The innkeeper looked around us, even though we were the only three people in the lobby, and still he lowered his voice as he admitted, "I believe my hotel is haunted."

"What? That can't be true. Surely you've been reading too many horror novels about hotels, and your imagination has supplied events you've been expecting to see," Momma said.

"That's not it, and it's not just me," he protested. "Things, unexplained things, have been happening ever since I bought the Overlook from its past owners. If this keeps up, I'm afraid I'm going to have to shut the place down and give it back to the bank."

"There's no need to panic just yet," I said. "Give us some specifics, and maybe we can help you figure this out."

"If only it were that easy," he said just as a man and woman, both somewhere in their late twenties, came into the inn and approached the main desk.

"Do you have any rooms available tonight?" the man asked brusquely.

"You don't have a reservation?" Mr. Garrett asked, though he'd told us earlier that we were the only new guests scheduled to arrive that day. If I had to guess, I'd say that he was keeping up appearances that his hotel was in demand. "I'm not sure what I can do on such short notice."

"I told you, Wesley," the woman said as she smacked her companion's arm. "You said they'd have plenty of rooms this time of year. What would a phone call have cost you? Now we need to drive around looking for someplace else to stay, and it's getting cold out there."

"I believe I could manage to find a room for you," Mr. Garrett said with some reluctance. He was really good at playing his part, I had to give him that much.

"We need *two* rooms," the girl said decidedly. "I'm not about to share a room with my brother. I'd rather sleep in the car."

"If that's the way you want it, far be it from me to stand in your way, Sis. Here you go," Wesley said as he offered her the keys. "Have fun trying not to freeze to death."

"I'm sure that won't be necessary," Mr. Garrett said. "I'm certain I can find accommodations for both of you."

"That would be great," the young woman said, and then she glanced over at us. "Wesley, you cut right in front of them, and they were here first. If anyone gets a room, they should be the ones to get it."

"Thanks, but we're already checked in," I said. "We were just chatting with Mr. Garrett."

"Who might Mr. Garrett be?" she asked.

"That would be me," the hotel owner said, trying again to smile but only partially succeeding.

"Nice to meet you, Mr. Garrett. I'm Nicole Langford, and this is my brother, Wesley," she said with a smile.

"Can we dispense with the chitchat and check in now?" Wesley asked petulantly. It was clear he was used to getting his way, and as gruff as he was, his sister was that friendly. "I'm sure you can finish your conversation later," he told us, dismissing us by turning his back on both Momma and me as he pulled out his wallet and started sorting through his credit cards.

"We'll continue this chat later," I told the innkeeper.

"It's really not necessary," Mr. Garrett said.

"As a matter of fact, I believe that it is," I countered with a smile.

"Very well," he replied, sighing slightly as he did so. "Would you like someone to help you to your room with your bags?" He looked around the space, but if there was a bellman on duty, I hadn't seen him yet. I had a feeling it was another example of the brave front Mr. Garrett was trying to put on to make it seem as though he was running a healthy and vibrant inn and not a hostelry on the verge of bankruptcy.

"Thanks, but we can manage just fine on our own," I said. I started to lift our bags off the cart when Momma said, "Suzanne, we might as well use this trolley, since we're coming right back down to the lobby after we deliver our bags."

"We are?" I asked her. If we'd had plans, she'd failed to mention them to me.

"We are," Momma said softly as we pulled far enough away from the others so we wouldn't be overheard. "We need to find an old map, and I have an idea where we might look now that Phillip's computer is missing."

"Okay then," I said. "Let's put these bags in our rooms and then take another walk. You know, we could drive, if you'd rather."

"No, I think a stroll around town is in order," Momma said. "It might help us get to know the place."

I wasn't about to argue the point. We pushed the cart to the elevator, stowed our bags in our respective rooms, and then brought the cart back downstairs so the Langfords could use it, if they needed it, at any rate. They still hadn't managed to check into their rooms yet, though they'd had plenty of time, at least as far as I was concerned.

Wesley was actually dickering with the hotel owner over his room rate, and Nicole shot us an apologetic look as we passed them. From the clothes the pair of them were wearing, I had a feeling they could afford to book the entire inn for the night with pocket change, but I knew enough wealthy people to realize that some of them were reluctant to part with a single dime, let alone a dollar.

Once Momma and I stepped back outside in the brisk afternoon air, we both instinctively tightened our jackets. There was no doubt it was getting chillier, and I hated the thought that anyone might be outside in it tonight.

"It's a bit sharp out, isn't it?" Momma asked.

"Have you changed your mind about the ride?" I asked with a grin.

"No, you know me; I love the cold. It's invigorating, isn't it?"

"Well, I can hardly complain after that, can I?" I asked happily.

"You seem to be in a particularly good mood this afternoon," she said as we started off.

"Imagine that. Why shouldn't I be?" I asked happily. "By the way, where exactly are we going?"

"I thought another trip to the library might be in order," she answered.

"I didn't think Phillip wanted us asking questions there in case someone might get suspicious," I reminded her.

"Suzanne, you know as well as I do that there are more ways to get information than by approaching someone directly. If I've learned anything helping you with some of your past investigations, it is that sometimes subterfuge is in order."

I grinned at her. "I always knew it. I just wasn't sure that you approved of deceit."

"We aren't really hurting anyone with a bit of mild deception," she said. "That's where I draw the line, though. I won't cause someone pain if it is at all possible to avoid it."

"Believe me, I feel the same way," I said. As we walked, I added, "Do you still want to know the real reason why I'm happy?"

"Is it because of the treasure hunt?" she asked.

"I suppose that's part of it, but the truth is, I'm just thrilled to be in the mountains with my family," I admitted. "Finding the Star is almost going to be a bonus."

Momma put her arm in mine and squeezed. "I can't tell you how much I appreciate the sentiment, but don't let Phillip hear you say that. This relic has become an obsession with him over the past six months. I think he's been using it to get over his recent difficulties."

"Is that what the crazy kids are calling cancer these days?" I asked her. "It was quite a bit more than a difficulty, and we both know it."

She nodded. "I believe he's hoping that we will all forget that it ever happened now that he's recovered from his surgery. You know, there were only a few people he told, and he confessed to me on the drive up that he was happy now that he'd kept it to himself."

"He should know that having cancer isn't anything to be ashamed of," I told her.

"Of course he does," Momma said, "but he doesn't want to be defined by the experience. Finding the Southern Shooting Star would be the mark he leaves on the world long after he's gone."

"But he's not expecting to go anytime soon, is he?" I asked, wondering if further test results had shown more than I'd been told.

"Not that we're aware of, but still, you can't blame him for thinking about his own mortality. He needs this, and I'm going to do everything in my power to make certain that he gets it. I gave him my word."

A declaration like that from my mother was something that might as well have been chiseled in stone. She took her word more seriously than most folks took written contracts. "Thanks for inviting us along for the hunt, then," I said.

"I was all for it, but actually, it was my husband's idea to invite the two of you. He really does care for you, Suzanne."

I knew that, but I didn't really like to talk about it all that much. "You know I feel the same way about him," I said, and then I felt as though it was time to change the subject. "So, how exactly are we going to pry this secret information from the librarian?"

"I thought we'd just ask," Momma said with a smile.

"What was that you said earlier about subterfuge?" I asked her with a grin.

"Our backstory is that we're researching our family's genealogy, and apparently there was a family of Parsonses in the area at one point in time."

Parsons was my mother's maiden name. When Momma had been a young girl, her father had died after a tractor had turned over on him. Her mother had remarried, but when her brand-new stepfather had offered to adopt her, Momma had steadfastly refused. She told me once that she'd cared for the new man in her mother's life, but he would never be a substitute for her own father.

"Is that even true?" I asked her. "Were there any Parsonses around here?"

"Who knows? The point is that we need information from the sixties, preferably a map that will show us the town's layout back then. My story will be that that's the only way we'll find out where they lived," Momma replied. "I'll say that from what I've been told, it was on the same street as the old library, so naturally we'd love to see that particular area while we're in town on another matter with our spouses. What do you think? Will it work?"

"It just might," I said with a grin. "Actually, that's quite neat. When did you think of that approach?"

"Phillip has been delving into his own genealogy as of late, so it seemed like a natural segue to me."

"It's clever, and it has the added bonus of having the plausibility that it might actually be true," I said. "Maybe *you* should be leading my investigations from here on out."

"No, I know when I'm in the presence of brilliance. I'd never dream of trying to take your place, Suzanne."

It was an odd compliment to get from my mother. "Did you just say brilliance?"

"I did," she affirmed. "Phillip and I have discussed your insights into the psyches of killers several times. It's an admirable trait, given your proclivity to investigate murder."

"It's not really a proclivity," I said. "I just can't stand to sit by and do nothing while a murderer might go free."

"Which is it then, are you standing, or are you sitting?" Momma asked, taking some of the serious tone from our conversation.

"Why can't it be a little bit of both?" I asked her. I loved getting compliments from my mother, about just about anything, truth be told, and I was sure that it would never fail to please me to earn her praise, but to have her comment favorably on my investigative prowess really warmed my soul and lifted my spirit.

After all, who doesn't like being told that they have a pretty baby?

After what seemed like a quick stroll through town, we were back where we'd been earlier.

There was one problem, though.

The library was closed.

Maybe we should have driven over after all.

At least then we might have made it in time.

Chapter 6

"I'M SORRY WE DIDN'T make it here in time, Suzanne. This is my fault," Momma said as we both stared at the hours posted on the library's front door.

"How is that even possible?" I asked her. "You didn't have anything to do with the operating hours of this place."

"No, but I was the one who wanted to walk here. If we'd driven, as you suggested, we would have been here in time to speak with someone," she told me.

"Don't beat yourself up, Momma. I was happy with the idea of walking, too," I reminded her. "Don't worry, we'll figure it out some other way."

We were about to turn to leave when I heard a noise behind us.

A trim young woman in her early thirties who was dressed smartly in a tweed suit and sporting a mass of luxurious black hair pulled back away from her face was coming out of the library's main entrance. She started locking the doors behind her as she saw us. She was balancing a few books in her arms while she tried to do it, and I was about to step in and offer to help hold them when she said, "I'm so sorry, but we close early on Wednesday nights," she said. "We'll be reopening at nine tomorrow morning, though, and I'd be more than happy to help you with anything you'd like then." She glanced at her watch, and then she frowned for a moment. "You know what? I've got a few minutes before I have to get home. Was there something I could help you with?"

It was time to make a decision. Either we went with Momma's lie, or we came clean and asked the librarian outright for a map of town. I immediately liked this woman, and I didn't really have the heart to outright lie to her.

Evidently my mother didn't have that problem. "My people used to live around here, and I'd love to see where they settled for a time," she said. "By the way, I'm Dot, and this is Suzanne."

"Hi," she said, trying and fighting in vain with the idea of shaking our hands, given the fact that her arms were still full. "I'm Leslie Ann."

"It's nice to meet you," I said.

"Do you have any idea where exactly it was that they lived?" she asked as I finally managed to take the stack of books from her. Leslie Ann took out her keys again and started to reopen the building, just for us. I felt a little bad about deceiving her, but Phillip had been right. It was important that we stayed under everyone's radar as long as we could manage it. Folks around Devil's Ridge probably didn't realize that they'd been hiding a treasure all these years, and if they found out what we were up to, it was most likely going to end badly for us, I was pretty sure of that.

"On the same street as the *old* library, I believe," Momma said as she glanced at the new facility.

"Seriously? You're kidding, right?" Leslie Ann asked incredulously.

"Why do you say that?" Momma asked.

I could hear a bit of panic creeping into her voice, so I decided to step in. "The new facility wasn't built on the grounds of the old one, was it?" I asked her.

"No, it's three streets over," she said.

"Then why were you surprised when my mother mentioned it?" I asked her.

"It just so happens that I live three doors down from the old library myself," she admitted as she locked the door again for the second time in four minutes. "You can walk with me over there right now, unless you have a car."

"We do, but it's at the Overlook Inn, where we're staying tonight," I said. "We'd be delighted to keep you company on your walk home, if you're sure you don't mind." She reached for her books once her keys were back in her purse, but I declined to return them. "I'd be happy to carry them for you if you'd like."

"I appreciate the offer, but I don't mind," she said.

I wasn't about to argue with her, but as I handed the books over to her, I couldn't help but notice the titles.

They were all centered around the Civil War.

That couldn't just be a coincidence, given why we were in town.

"That's a fascinating topic you're researching," I said, trying not to give my excitement away as we headed toward her home. Momma's eyes grew big as she saw the reading material herself. I just hoped she could keep it together and not give anything away.

"The truth of the matter is that I've never been all that interested in the subject before, but a young couple about my age came in earlier asking about lost Confederate gold, and it made me curious." Apparently not everyone was as worried about keeping a low profile as we were. Leslie Ann grinned at us slightly before continuing. "That's a research librarian's curse, a case of massive curiosity. I start researching things for our patrons, and then I get wrapped up in the topic myself. It's a wonder I get anything done around here at all."

I didn't even need to ask who the couple was who'd come in asking questions, though I was certain that if Wesley and Nicole Langford heard themselves described as a couple, neither one of them would have been pleased. "What exactly did they want to know?"

"Just some general information, mostly," she admitted. "The funny thing was that I got the impression that neither one of them had spent much time in a library before today, and they were searching for information about two of the most disparate topics you could imagine."

I had a feeling it concerned bad guys from the sixties, but I wasn't sure that we should show that much interest in what they'd been researching.

Clearly Momma had other ideas, though. "How fascinating. What else were they looking for?"

"I suppose there's no harm in telling you. After all, it's not exactly doctor–patient confidentiality," she said. "They wanted to know about gangsters of the twentieth century. That I could tell them all about without having to look it up." I looked at her oddly, as did Momma. "You're not from around here, so of course you wouldn't know, but the notorious gangster Thomas 'Tommy Gun' Malone was arrested less than a mile from where we're standing at this very moment. It's our own little claim to fame, even though it happened back in the sixties."

"Wow, that's incredible," I said.

"I know, right?" she asked. "Anyway, I told them I'd do a little more digging into the lost gold angle and let them know tomorrow when they came back by the library."

"You're quite accommodating, especially since you said they were both strangers around here," Momma said approvingly.

"Anyone seeking knowledge is my friend," Leslie Ann said loftily. After a second, she grinned. "That sounded much more officious than I meant it to. It's just that it was a relief doing the work of an actual research librarian. That's where my training lies, not that I don't love my job now. It's just nice to be able to sink my teeth into the meat of a question, you know?" She shook herself for a moment and then smiled again. "Here I am blathering on and on about myself. Tell me about the two of you. My mother always used to tell me that you never learn anything if you're the only one doing the talking."

"Our husbands are here on business, and we tagged along," I volunteered.

"Are you two best friends?" Leslie Ann asked. "You are, aren't you? I have a sense about these things."

I was about to tell the librarian our real status when Momma said something that almost made me cry. "Suzanne is indeed my best friend in the world," she said proudly. "It also gives me great pleasure to say that she is my only child as well."

"Thanks, Momma," I said, touching her shoulder lightly.

"I envy you," Leslie Ann said a bit wistfully.

"Aren't you and your mother close, child?" Momma asked her. It might have sounded presumptuous or even condescending coming from anyone else, but from my mother, it was an earnest and heartfelt question asked with the best of intentions.

"She passed away when I was twelve," Leslie Ann said. "I have some great memories of our time together, which is more than I can say for my little brother, but I missed having a mom of my own, you know?"

Momma touched her hand lightly. "I do. I lost my father at a young age as well, so I can at least imagine some of your pain."

"Then you know what a hole it leaves in your life," she said as she wiped away a single tear. "I never expected to have such an emotional walk home today."

"I'm so sorry," Momma said. "I didn't mean to pry."

"You didn't," Leslie Ann said, grinning slightly to prove that she meant it. "I believe that a little tear every now and then is good for you. Well, we're here," she added as she pointed to a run-down old building with a brick wall that was in a terrible state of disrepair. "It's hard to believe that in three days, this will all be gone."

"What do you mean?" I asked her.

"It's been set to be demolished to make way for a new hotel," she said. "Some developer from out of state bought the building and the land around it ages ago, and he's evidently finally ready to get started." She paused and then asked, "By the way, I forgot to ask you. What was your family's name? Do you happen to remember their exact address?"

"It is Parsons," Momma said, telling the complete and utter truth. "As to where they lived, I'm afraid that is hard to say."

Okay, that was a big fat whopping lie, but I wasn't going to hold it against her.

"Then I'd like to think that perhaps they lived where I am now," she said with a firm nod. "Would you like to come in and look around the old place?" She glanced at her watch and then added, "I have a few minutes before I have to get ready for my date."

"We won't bother you any more," Momma said. "You've been more than helpful as it is. Thank you for your hospitality."

She nodded. "I was happy to do it."

"I have one more question for you, if you have a second," I told Leslie Ann as she started up her own walk.

"Sure. I'll answer it if I can."

"Does Devil's Ridge really need *two* hotels?" I asked her.

"Honestly, it can barely support one. Poor Jimmy. I've known him forever. We even dated a few times in high school before I blew it. He put everything he had into the Overlook. Everyone knows that he's mortgaged to the hilt, and since he's taken over, it's been nothing but bad luck for him. Now comes some mysterious developer that's surely going to wipe him out, and there's not a thing he can do about it. It's so sad."

"I'm sure it is," Momma said. "Well, we won't keep you any longer."

"It's been a real pleasure," the librarian said as she headed toward her front porch. "Stop in tomorrow if you get the chance. It was nice meeting you."

"You as well," Momma and I said in unison, something that made Leslie Ann laugh.

"Wow, that was an informative conversation," I said as we headed back toward the hotel, which just happened to be past the library's former building. "Talk about good timing."

"It was fortuitous that we caught her as she was leaving," Momma said as she stared at the old building and, more importantly, the broken-down brick wall in question.

"I'm talking about them tearing this all down in three days," I said. "If Phillip had been just a little bit slower with his research, we'd have been out of luck."

"My husband is very good at what he does," Momma said proudly. "As is my daughter."

"Gosh, I wasn't sure you even *liked* my donuts," I answered with a grin.

"I do, but you know that wasn't what I was talking about. You're easy to talk to, aren't you, Suzanne? That's what makes you such a good investigator."

"If I am, it's all because my mother taught me how to listen, how to really listen, at a very early age," I said as I looked at the crumbling wall. There were vines against its base, and brush had grown up to nearly disguise the structure completely in places. I found myself counting rows and columns from where the old lion must have been perched all those years, but I kept losing my count.

At least the bricks in the general proximity of where we needed to look appeared to be intact, though the mortar was failing in several places all around it.

"Should we just walk over and start looking for the Star ourselves?" I asked as I began to take a step toward the wall.

Momma put a hand on my shoulder. "Not with prying eyes watching our every move," she said, glancing back over her shoulder.

I looked as well and saw an old woman with frizzled gray hair peering out the window at us. She wasn't even trying to hide the fact that she was watching us intently.

"You're right," I said as I pivoted and started back the way we'd just come. It took everything I had not to wave good-bye to the woman, but I knew that we were trying to keep a low profile, so I restrained myself.

As we walked, Momma said, "I'll wager that she's at that window every waking hour."

"Then we'll have to come back in the middle of the night when she's asleep," I said. "I'm willing to bet that the men won't have any problem skulking around in the dark."

Momma smiled. "Are you kidding? I honestly believe that will just serve to enhance the experience for them."

"You're probably right," I said as I rubbed my hands together. "I can't believe how cold it's getting, Momma."

"Then let's hurry back to the inn before we *both* freeze to death," she answered. "That's terrible bad luck Mr. Garrett is having, isn't it?" she added as we both picked up our pace.

"If it's luck at all," I admitted.

"What do you mean?" Momma asked me.

"Think about it. Someone's clearly trying to drive him out of business, at least if we discount this haunted angle he's so intent on, and then there's news of a new hotel coming to town, just as the Overlook is in dire straits. It's all a bit too coincidental for my taste."

"Suzanne, coincidences have been known to happen, you know."

"I know, but they make me suspicious, anyway," I said.

It seemed to be a lot farther going back to the inn than it had been coming from it, and I had to wonder if we'd ever make it back when I spotted the lights of the inn from just down the road.

"I don't know about you, but I could use something to warm me up," Momma said.

"You read my mind," I admitted. "Which do you prefer, hot chocolate or coffee? Unless you had something a bit stronger in mind."

"I did not," Momma said firmly. "I was thinking about coffee, but I believe I like your idea of hot chocolate better still."

"Then let's go see if the Overlook can satisfy our wishes," I said as I put my arm in my mother's and walked her the rest of the way back to our hotel.

Chapter 7

OUR MEN WERE WAITING for us in the lobby, and I had a chance to look around a bit as we joined them. The hardwood floors of the Overlook were old and a bit battered, but I doubted it would take much to bring them back to their previous glory. There were leather-covered benches and chairs in the nearby lounge, all centered toward and focused on the massive stone fireplace with a large wooden mantel that appeared to have been salvaged from an old barn. A welcome fire crackled and popped in the fireplace, but I noticed that there weren't many folks enjoying it.

Momma and I nodded in Jimmy Garrett's direction. He offered us a sad little smile before he went back to the ledger book he was studying.

"That heat feels amazing," I said as I warmed myself with the radiant warmth emanating from the hearth.

"I love the crackle of the fire as it burns," Momma said. She then turned to the men. "How did you two manage to get along without us?"

"It was difficult, but we somehow survived," Phillip said with a slight smile.

"Well, don't keep us on pins and needles. Tell us what you've been up to," Momma said.

"First things first. The truck should be ready by tomorrow at noon," he explained. "They were more than eager to help us out."

"Once you flashed your badge," Jake said with a slight smile.

"I told you before. I didn't mean to," Phillip protested, but it was half-hearted at best. "It just popped out."

"I can see how that might happen," Jake said, now having to fight harder to hide his smile.

"And what about the chief of police?" I asked Jake, who started staring into the fire.

"It's sheriff, actually," he said as his gaze returned to me, "and we never got to meet him."

"Why not?" Momma asked. "Was he tied up with a big case?"

"As a matter of fact, he's in Florida on vacation, trying to get away from the cold," Jake answered.

"Did you at least get to speak with his second-in-command about the robbery?" I asked.

"He was out of the office making his rounds, but we managed to arrange breakfast here with him tomorrow morning," Jake said.

"For the three of us," Phillip added, as if he'd needed to make it clear that Momma and I weren't invited.

"All in all, I can't really say that we accomplished all that much," Jake supplied. "What did you two do while we were gone?"

"Who, us? Not much. Oh, you might be interested in this. While you men were out taking care of manly business, Momma and I found the site of the old library," I said with a grin.

"What? How did you manage to do that? You didn't tell anyone why we were here, did you?" Phillip asked, clearly alarmed by our new information.

"No. Momma was amazing," I told them both. "We met the librarian for Devil's Ridge, a nice young woman named Leslie Ann, and she led us to the old building herself."

"What story did you give her to manage that kind of royal treatment?" Jake asked, looking carefully at me.

"Momma handled it," I explained as I turned to her. "You tell them."

My mother looked pleased by the praise. "I just mentioned that I had family from here, and we were looking for their former house. When I said that it was near the old library, which we hadn't been able to find, she volunteered to walk us over there herself. It turns out that she lives a few houses down from the old library."

"Then let's not waste any more time and go get that...item," Phillip said as he started to stand.

"Not so fast," I told him. "It's complicated."

Phillip settled back down into his seat as a frown crossed his lips. "Of course it is. What's going on?"

"The old library and the brick wall in front of it are both set to be bulldozed in a few days, but that's not the immediate issue. There's an older woman who lives across from the abandoned building who watched us the entire time we were there. We're going to have to go back in the dead of night if we have the slightest chance of searching that brick wall without someone watching us."

"We can do that," Phillip said as he whistled softly. "I can't believe we came so close to missing it all. Why are they tearing the old library down, anyway?"

I lowered my voice. "Apparently someone wants to build a new hotel here in town."

"What about this place?" Jake asked.

"That's the other thing. We had a chat with Jimmy Garrett after you two left. He thinks the place is legitimately haunted."

"You're kidding," Jake said. "Did he happen to say why?"

"We didn't have a chance to get into it, but it turns out that he's not just the manager here. He owns the place, or at least the bit that the bank doesn't still own. If things don't turn around here, and I mean quickly, he could lose it all."

"And how is that *our* problem, exactly?" Phillip asked us. "We're here for another reason, remember?"

"I'm not likely to forget it," I said, "but if someone needs our help, have we ever turned them away before? I'm a bit surprised in you, Phillip. It's not like you to be so cold. What happened, did you get gold fever, and nothing else matters anymore?"

"No. Of course not. I'm sorry. You're absolutely right. I'm just so excited about finding an artifact that the whole world thought was gone for good. Of course we'll help Garrett if we can," Phillip said.

That was more like the man I'd grown to know over the years he'd been with my mother. She must have thought so, too, because she reached over and touched her husband's shoulder lightly. It wasn't much as far as gestures went, but it was clearly enough for him.

"You know, there's no reason we can't look for the Star *and* help Garrett," Jake told Phillip, obviously trying to comfort him.

"I know. I'm not sure what's gotten into me lately. Ever since I found that reference to the Star, I've been a little crazy."

"Don't kid yourself. Gold fever is a very real thing," I said. "Anyway, there's more, and you're both going to want to hear this. Leslie Ann told us that a pair of strangers was at the library looking for information on two subjects. Any guesses as to who it was, and what they might have been looking into?"

"You're kidding," Jake said.

"Kidding about what?" Phillip asked. "Am I missing something?" After a moment, he nodded. "I don't believe it. Wesley and Nicole Langford aren't in town hoping to have a nice and quiet vacation."

"From her descriptions of them, I have no doubt that it was indeed the two of them," Momma said.

"And they were looking into gangsters and Civil War treasures," Jake said dully. "Tell me I'm wrong about that."

"I wish I could," I said to him, "but I make it a policy not to lie to you."

"As a general rule, I'd have to say that's a good policy for you to have," Jake said with a flashing grin in my direction. He then turned to my stepfather. "Phillip, how could they possibly know about this? I was under the impression that the fact that the Star was in Devil's Ridge was some kind of big secret."

"I thought it was, but don't forget, there was another person trying to buy Tommy Gun's letters besides me," he said glumly. "They might have known the general area to search but not specifics."

"How could they have known even that?" Momma asked.

"It just makes sense, when you look at it," Phillip told her. "Tommy was arrested not far from the library, so it's not that big a stretch to believe that he'd stash something nearby for safekeeping if he realized that he was about to be caught."

"I can see that, but how did anyone but his sister learn what he'd done?" she asked them.

"Dot, there's not a lot to do in prison," Jake told her. "Guys have a tendency to talk, especially if they're bragging. He could have hinted about what he'd done to any number of people without giving too many specifics away." Jake turned to Phillip. "You don't happen to know how Tommy Gun died, do you? Was it a lingering illness, or was it maybe something more sudden?"

"It was pretty sudden, all right. Someone shoved a shiv between his ribs at mealtime," Phillip admitted. "I doubt that he saw it coming. When Tommy found out that his sister had just died, he got surly, and two days later, he talked back to the wrong man."

"So he probably didn't have a chance to tell anyone else where he'd hid the Star," I said.

"I don't know about that. He had two days," Phillip said.

"Two days in grief over the loss of his sister," I reminded him. "I doubt he was in any kind of mood to tell any of his secrets to someone else."

"Probably not," Phillip conceded. A thought clearly suddenly occurred to him. "Wesley and Nicole must have been the ones who broke into my truck."

"Not necessarily," Jake said.

My stepfather looked at him askance for a moment before he spoke again. "Don't tell me you believe it was a coincidence that I was robbed practically the moment we got to town."

"No, but what makes us think that the six of us are the *only* ones around here looking for the Star?" he asked. "After all, *we* all found out about it. What about the idea that a local has been looking for the treasure all along, and suddenly they see an influx of tourists when there's really no reason for them to be here? If they think *one* of us is getting close, they might make a preemptive strike to see exactly what we know. I'd be curious to know if the Langfords have had any trouble with the locals themselves since they've been in town."

"I don't know, but I don't really want to ask them, do you?" I asked.

"Let me think about it," Jake said. Since he'd left the state police, he'd come to terms with working without any authority backing him up. No one was compelled to tell him anything, which had been a really difficult thing to swallow at first. It had been a tough transition for him, but he was now handling it beautifully.

"In the meantime, I was promised hot chocolate, and I'm determined to get a mug of it," I said as I stood and headed off in search of the inn's restaurant. "Are you all coming?"

"We're right behind you," Momma said.

The restaurant was everything I'd expected, matching the lobby and the reception area to a tee, from the dark décor to the faded and worn look of everything around us. Even the tablecloths and other linens had seen better days, washed again and again until they barely managed to hang together. The waiter taking care of us looked as though he'd been there for the hotel's grand opening a hundred years earlier. Okay, that was an exaggeration, but I honestly feared for him as he made his way over to us with a shuffling gait that made me wonder if he'd survive serving tonight's meal, let alone last one more night.

Then something surprising happened. As he faced us, his somber expression was interrupted by an unexpected smile, and there was a glint in his eye that made me think this was all a game to him as he stepped up his pace to an exaggerated strut. "Fooled you all, didn't I?" he asked merrily.

"You did, but why?" Momma asked him.

"It's a game I like to play with new folks at the Overlook. I call it 'Expectations.' Most folks see an old man in his eighties, and they just assume he's got one foot in the grave with the other not far behind, so I like to shake them up a bit. Shoot, my dad lived to be 103, and he would have made it to 104 if he hadn't tried driving on that icy road last Christmas so he wouldn't miss church. I offered to drive him myself, but he wouldn't hear of it. So, what can I start you folks off with tonight?"

"What's good?" I asked, a question that usually elicited some kind of response from the server.

The server seemed to ponder the question with more intensity than I'd expected. "The steak's okay, but Manny tends to overcook them, so you're on your own there. The baked chicken is pretty good, and so is the pot roast, but if you order the fish, I'll do my best to talk you out of it. Shoot, I might not even bring it to the table, so consider yourself warned."

It was more information than I'd ever gotten from a server ever before, and I knew that he'd just earned a more-than-generous tip from my husband. Jake respected candor and honesty above just about everything else.

I smiled at our waiter and said, "I'm Suzanne, and this is my husband, Jake, my mother, Dot, and my stepfather, Phillip."

He grinned broadly. "Pleased to meet you all. I'm Joy."

"Joy? Is that your name, or is it what you try to bring to the folks around you?" I asked him, laughing a bit as I said it.

"The honest truth is that it's a little of both. They started calling me that as a kid, and it just kind of stuck. My real name is Julian Othello

Yount, or Joy for short. At least it's better than my twin brother's nickname."

The question was just waiting to be asked, so Phillip did it for the rest of us. "What do they call him?"

"Late for dinner, every single time," the man named Joy said and then happily laughed at his own joke.

"Do you even have a twin brother?" Momma asked him, clearly taken in by his charm as well.

"Sure I do. His name is Herbert Elliot Young, so whenever anyone wants him, they just yell, 'Hey.' Now that we've all been introduced, may I take your orders?"

"I think I'll have the fish," I said with a grin.

The man named Joy was about to protest when he saw my smile. "Just for that, that's what I'm going to tell Manny you want."

I pretended to act hurt. "You wouldn't do that to me, would you? After all, I thought we were friends."

He nodded to Jake and smiled. "You've got your hands full with this young lady, don't you, sir?"

"I won't deny it," Jake said, but before I could protest, he added, "But I wouldn't trade my time with her for anything in the world."

"I know exactly what you mean. My wife passed away last year after we'd been married forty-two years, and there's not a day goes by that I don't miss her." Joy's smile faded for a moment, and then the spark came back in full. "But I still cherish every last memory." He looked around and saw that Mr. Garrett was watching the exchange curiously. "Now, if you don't mind, let me take your order while the boss is looking over my shoulder. I'd hate to get fired at my age. I'm too old to do much else than this. At least that's what folks around here think."

"If they do, then it is clear that they would be wrong," Momma said.

"I appreciate that," Joy replied.

After we ordered—no fish or steak—he ambled over to the drink station at a much more brisk pace than he'd used approaching our table initially.

"That's how I want to be when I grow up," Jake said with a smile.

"Keep it up," I told him as I patted his hand. "You're well on your way."

"I hope you're right," he answered.

I looked over at my stepfather, who had been quiet for a bit too long for my taste. "This is killing you just sitting here while that relic is out there waiting for you in the dark, isn't it?" I asked him softly.

"What? No, that wasn't what I was thinking about at all. The truth is that I'm a bit disappointed in myself for discounting Mr. Garrett's problems because I'm so focused on what we're here to do."

"Phillip, don't be so hard on yourself," Momma said as she patted his hand. "You've been working on this for a very long time. Of course you're focused on recovering the er...item in question."

"Thanks, but it's still no excuse."

"We could always help Mr. Garrett and go back home *without* recovering the item," I said with a grin. "Would that ease your conscience any?"

That garnered a grin from my stepfather that showed he hadn't lost his sense of humor completely. "I don't know, and thankfully, we'll never find out. At this point, holding the Star in my hands is almost beside the point," Phillip said.

"Really? Then Jake and I will be glad to take it off your hands once we recover it," I added, doing my best to get him out of his sullen mood.

"I said 'almost,'" he reminded me with a full-fledged smile. "Jake's right. There's no reason we can't make the recovery and help Garrett out at the same time, if we can."

"Then it's settled," Momma said. "We will be treasure hunters *and* good Samaritans."

"That sounds like a busy couple of days to me, but I'm in," I answered.

"I am, too," Jake added as he touched my hand lightly with his. "I'm leading quite an adventurous life for a retired state police investigator," Jake said as Joy brought us our drinks and distributed them. The tray had wavered in his hand for a moment, but he quickly corrected it and then headed over to take care of another customer.

After our server was gone, Momma said, "Then it's settled. Which should we tackle first, the innkeeper or the item?"

Phillip did his best to restrain himself as he said, "It might be easier for us to focus on the problems here *after* we've done what we originally set out to do." He quickly added, "Unless you all want to do it the other way. I'm good with whatever the three of you decide."

Jake, Momma, and I all burst out laughing at the same time, and Phillip grinned good-naturedly at the teasing.

"Phillip, we'd never dream of doing that to you," Momma said. "After we eat, we'll work on our plan to recover the treasure."

"It doesn't have to be too intricate," Phillip said. "Either it's still there waiting for us, or someone else has already found it."

"We've got prying eyes watching us though, remember?" I told him.

"Well, it's dark out now, so I'm not sure how much she's really going to see," Phillip declared. "I say after we eat, we walk over to the old library and do what we came here to do, regardless of what anyone else might see."

"Maybe we should drive instead," I said, remembering how cold Momma and I had gotten walking back to the inn, and it had still been mostly light out then. It was hard to imagine how low the temperature had dropped since we'd come inside.

"Maybe we should do that," Momma said. "We can park near Leslie Ann's house and walk over to the library. She's out on a date, so I'm sure she won't mind."

"Then we've got a plan," Phillip said as I noticed Joy heading our way, both arms laden with plates of food.

"*After* we eat, though," I said with a smile.

"Oh, yes," Phillip echoed.

We were nearly finished with our meals when a dark note broke into our festive meal.

Wesley and Nicole Langford came into the dining room and searched the room quickly. It was obvious they were looking for someone in particular, and the moment they spotted us, they stormed toward our table with fire in both their gazes.

It appeared that they were nearly as unhappy with us as we were with them, though I didn't for the life of me have any idea why that might be true.

I suspected we were about to find out soon enough, though.

Chapter 8

"WE'RE GOING TO GIVE you a chance to explain yourself before we call the police, but you'd better make it good," Wesley said angrily as he stood over Phillip.

Jake hated being challenged, and his attitude was that the only way to deal with a bully was directly, and confrontationally, if necessary. As he stood up, he said icily, "Back off."

As Phillip stood to join him, Wesley took a step back. Momma and I stood as well, presenting a united front against the attack on our family.

"You're not going to get away with this," Wesley hissed. "Give it back to us, and we won't call the cops."

Nicole, in a much more appeasing voice, added, "Let's be reasonable, okay? There's no reason to draw attention to what we're doing here, is there? Let's be adults about it and see if we can resolve things without the police."

"That's going to be hard to do, since we're both former chiefs of police," Jake told them with a smile that carried no warmth in it whatsoever. I forgot sometimes how deadly serious my husband could be when the occasion called for it.

"I'm curious to know what it is that you believe was stolen, and more importantly, why are you so convinced that one of us did it?" Momma asked them.

"Is this really the time or the place to have this conversation?" Nicole asked. I looked around and saw that other diners were watching us. "Why don't we at least all sit so we're not attracting so much attention."

"I don't *want* to sit with them," Wesley snarled. "I want what was ours back again. I knew it was a waste of time just asking for it."

"We honestly don't know what you're talking about," I told them. It was a rare occasion indeed when mine was one of the voices of reason.

"Why are you targeting us?" Phillip asked, repeating Momma's question. "If someone stole something of yours, anyone could have done it."

"But they didn't, did they? The irony of it all is that we probably would have never known it was you if you hadn't been so sloppy," Wesley said as he produced an envelope from his pocket. "It must have fallen out of your pocket when you were searching our rooms."

Wesley Langford held a standard business envelope in the air in front of us, and after he showed us Phillip's name and address, he flipped it over and showed us some handwritten notes on the other side. "Don't try to deny it. This is your handwriting, isn't it?"

Phillip reached for the envelope, but Wesley snatched it back. "You can read it from there. I'm not letting go of the evidence."

My stepfather gave him an irritated look, and then he pulled out his reading glasses and studied the envelope from a few feet away. "It's mine all right, but I didn't leave it in your room."

"Do you honestly expect us to believe that?" Wesley asked.

"I don't really care what you believe. Someone broke into my truck not long after we got here by smashing a window and taking my notes as well as my computer. This was among the stolen papers they took."

Wesley didn't look pleased with our story, even though it was the truth. "Why should we believe you?"

"Call the body shop in town," Phillip said. "They're fixing my truck even as we speak." He glanced at his watch. "Forget that. They're closed, but first thing tomorrow morning, you can go down there and ask them yourselves."

"Wesley, surely they wouldn't break their own truck window just to set themselves up just in case they got caught doing something they didn't think anyone would know about," Nicole said soothingly.

"Even if all of that were true, it still doesn't explain how this envelope got in my room," he said, waving the paper around in the air again.

Mr. Garrett had to have noticed the confrontation. He approached us and asked softly, "Is there something I can help you folks with here?"

"No, everything's fine," Momma said as soothingly as she could manage.

"For now," Wesley admitted.

Garrett looked confused by our responses given what he'd just witnessed firsthand, but there really wasn't much else he could do about it if no one was going to tell him what was really going on. "Very well. If you need me, I'll be right over there," he said, pointing to the maître d' stand not more than a dozen feet away from our table.

"Thanks," I said as warmly as I could manage. The hotel owner had enough problems without having to worry about a break-in in one of his rooms, but I was afraid that we were only delaying the bad news. There was no way that Wesley Langford was going to be able to keep his mouth shut for very long. We just needed to make sure he didn't drag us into his story.

After the innkeeper was gone, Jake said calmly, "As to how that envelope got into your room, it's obvious, isn't it? Someone planted it there to make you think that *we* were behind the theft of whatever was so valuable to you."

"There's no way anybody is that smart. It sounds too complicated to me," Wesley said. "I like my version better."

"Well, we don't always get what we want, now do we?" I asked him. Just because Wesley didn't have the imagination to carry out that kind of plan didn't mean that someone else couldn't do it. "You didn't comment about what was written on the other side of that envelope," I said. It had only taken a second for me to see that Phillip had been making notes on the letters he'd bought from Tommy Gun's sister, and where he might find the Star. He must have written all of that before he'd cracked the code and learned that it was in the brick wall outside the old library. "That's kind of telling, isn't it?"

"What does it matter *what* was written there?" Wesley asked, clearly lying, and doing it badly at that. "His name and address was all that I needed."

"I might just believe you if I hadn't learned earlier today that you two have been snooping around the library looking for information about Tommy Gun Malone's time here, and also about lost gold from the Civil War."

"Maybe I'm just a history buff," Wesley protested.

"Maybe, but then why would you decide to research it only now? My guess is that you didn't realize that they were related topics until very recently." A sudden thought occurred to me. "How do we know that *you* weren't the ones who broke into my stepfather's truck? You could have failed to find what you were looking for, so you decided to use something you'd stolen to sidetrack us from our own quest."

"That's ridiculous," Wesley said.

"I'm not so sure," Nicole answered softly.

He spun around and stared angrily at his sister. "Surely you don't believe that *I* broke into *their* truck and stole something from *them*. When would I even have had the time? We were together all day."

"It wasn't *all* day, Wesley," she said, "but that's not what I'm saying. I'm just admitting that what happened could be spun more than one way." She took a deep breath and then added, "I don't care what you think. I'm telling them."

"You are not!" he shouted, his volume going up considerably.

"They already know we know, Wesley. Maybe we can work together," she reasoned.

"That's not going to happen," Wesley said loudly.

Mr. Garrett didn't want to lose six paying guests, so he was being overly cautious with us, but I knew if we got much louder, he'd have no choice but to come over again, and that was something that none of us wanted.

"Do what you want," Nicole told him, and then she turned to us. "You're looking for the Southern Shooting Star, too, aren't you?"

Phillip shrugged. "I don't know what you're talking about."

"Come on, work with me here," Nicole pled. "The notes on the envelope told us that *you* were the ones who bought those letters from Tommy to his sister that Henry was selling."

"They stole them, they didn't buy them," Wesley corrected her. "We were all set to pay a fair price when you swooped in at the last second and outbid us. At least you thought you did."

"What are you talking about?" Phillip asked, looking puzzled by his comment.

"Did you honestly think that lying jerk wouldn't make copies of everything he had so he could sell the same packet to us, too?"

"Even the coded letter?" I asked, blurting it out without thought.

"Coded letter? There was no coded letter!" Wesley snapped. "He cheated us," he told Nicole angrily. "Did he honestly think he'd get away with it?"

"As a matter of fact, the odds were pretty good," she admitted a bit glumly. "Think about it, Wesley. What are the chances we'd ever compare notes with the people who actually bought the original packet?"

"What did the coded letter say?" Wesley insisted. "We have every bit as much right to that information as you do."

"I suggest you take that up with Henry," Phillip said.

"Not a chance. If we leave town now, you're going to grab the Star, and we'll be out of luck. You're not about to get rid of us that easily."

Jake said, "Do what you want, but we're not sharing *anything* with you."

"Thanks for the suggestion, though," I said to Nicole. She'd been trying to be reasonable, and even though we weren't going to take her up on her offer to combine forces in our search, there was no reason to take it out on her.

"Sure, no problem. I was just trying to smooth things over," she replied.

"I've told you a thousand times, it's not your job to make things easier for me, Nicole," Wesley snapped. "This is clearly a waste of time," he said as he suddenly stood.

"If you're calling the police, we'd love to be included on the call," Phillip said with a smile.

Wesley looked at him unhappily. "I've heard all about how cops stick up for other cops. I'm not about to bring them into this. You should know that it's personal now, though. So, just to be clear, you're not going to return what you stole from us?"

"We already told you," Phillip said with a hint of anger in his voice. "We didn't steal anything from you. If you took our things, I'd like them back myself, especially my laptop."

"Sorry, but I can't help you, either," Wesley said with a quick shake of his head. "Come on, Nicole. Let's get out of here."

She looked at us, shrugged, and then she got up to join her brother.

Before they could leave our table area though, Jake asked, "By the way, what are you two driving?"

"That's none of your business," Wesley snapped.

"It's a red Lexus convertible," Nicole answered even as her brother began to give her a dirty look.

"Why did you tell them that?" he asked her with a whine.

"How hard would it be for them to find out?" she asked before looking back at Jake. "Why do you want to know?"

"Just curious," Jake answered.

"I kind of doubt that," she said, but then she smiled slightly. "Anyway, you all have a good night."

"You, too," Momma said.

"Come on, Nicole. Let's see if this town has any decent food that's not grossly overpriced like the rooms here are." He wanted Mr. Garrett to hear his snide comment, and it scored a double hit from the expression on the innkeeper's face. Some people just couldn't resist taking shots at other folks, even when there was no reason for it.

When it came right down to it, I guess they were just unhappy people who loved spreading their misery around to anyone who would take it.

"Hey, I just realized something," I said as soon as they were gone.

"What's that?" Jake asked.

"I never got my hot chocolate," I said.

"Should we order some now?" Momma asked.

"I'm not sure I'm still in the mood for any at the moment," I admitted. "They kind of put a damper on our little party, didn't they?"

"They certainly sped up our timetable a bit," Phillip said as he signaled our server and made signs that he was ready for the check.

"What do you mean?" Momma asked him.

"We now know for a fact that someone else is in town looking for the Star," he said softly. "If it's still in that brick wall, we need to find it before anyone else does."

"Do you mean right now?" Momma asked him incredulously.

"You don't have to come if you don't want to, Dot. I know how cold it is outside, but I'm afraid this won't even wait a few more hours."

"But they never got the coded letter," I said. "They have no idea where to look."

"They don't have it *yet*, you mean," Jake said. "I agree with Phillip. I'm guessing Wesley is talking to that weasel who sold the papers to two different people right now, demanding everything in the set, including the coded letter. I'm fairly certain he'll have to pay more to get it, but does he seem like the type of man to be stymied by money, particularly when he feels as though he's about to lose something he clearly so desperately wants?"

"It's not a game, Jacob," Momma said.

"All due respect, Dot, but that's exactly what this is, and I don't mean to lose, either."

Phillip nodded. "Then it's settled. You two head back upstairs, and Jake and I will run our little errand."

"Who said I wasn't coming along, too?" I asked them, using a deadly sweet tone that I was sure both men would recognize. They were about to move into dangerous territory, and they at least deserved fair warning before they triggered a response from me that I was sure neither one of them would like.

Momma saw what was happening and headed the fight off before it could even get started. "Of course we're all going to do this together," she said. "Let's pay our check, and then we'll proceed, full steam ahead."

I nodded. "That sounds like a plan to me, Momma." Then I turned to both men, each in their own turn. "Any objections?"

"No, ma'am," they said in perfect, almost rehearsed unity.

I patted both their hands. "Good boys."

We were still waiting to pay our check when, to my surprise, Mr. Garrett came back to our table instead of Joy.

What was this about?

Chapter 9

"I COULDN'T HELP BUT overhear some of that," the inn's owner said as he neared our table. "I truly hate to have discord at the Overlook."

"I don't blame you one bit," I said quickly, trying to appease him. "We weren't looking for trouble, but Wesley Langford accused us of doing something that we didn't do, and we felt we needed to defend ourselves. Surely you understand that."

"I suppose," he said with a hint of a frown. "Can I expect any *more* trouble between you all?"

"I wouldn't be surprised one bit," Jake said firmly. "But I can promise you that *we* won't go looking for trouble. As a matter of fact, we'll avoid it if we can, but I can't speak for the Langfords. It's really up to them, but we won't be pushed around by anyone."

Mr. Garrett took that in. "That's all I can ask of you. I wouldn't expect any man or woman to be a doormat for anyone else, but I don't want my other guests disturbed."

Momma looked around the dining room. "Honestly, no one else appears to be disturbed, Mr. Garrett. We were most careful to keep things low-key. I know this is the last thing in the world you need right now, and all I can say is that if we can keep from adding to your troubles, we will."

He physically shrank into himself a bit when he heard that. "You heard the news, didn't you? Of course you did. Why am I surprised that it's all over town?"

"Which particular piece of news are you talking about?" I asked him. I'd learned long ago not to volunteer information if I could help it. After all, we could be talking about two different things, though I doubted it.

"Someone's building a competing hotel in town," he said. "They're going to drive me out of business one way or the other."

"That's what we heard," I admitted. "It's an odd thing though, isn't it? After all, the Overlook seems to be all that Devil's Ridge really needs."

"Once upon a time, it was more than enough," he said, "but with everything that's been going on in the past month, I'm not sure how long that might still be true. Maybe I should do what my friends are urging me to do and sell out while I can. I have two more days until the offer I got for the place is gone forever. It's less than what I paid for it, but at least I'd be free of the place once and for all. To be honest with you, I'm not sure why I'm holding on to it anymore." When he looked around though, it was clear to me why he was doing it.

The Overlook was obviously more than just a hotel to him.

It was home.

"If you don't want to sell out, then don't do it," I said rashly.

"Suzanne, perhaps there are factors of which we aren't aware," Momma said, scolding me.

"Maybe, but you taught me long ago not to let myself be bullied into doing *anything* I didn't already want to do. If that advice was good enough for your daughter, why shouldn't it apply to everyone?"

"I'm sorry, I didn't mean to start a family squabble," Mr. Garrett said. "The main reason I came by was to offer you tonight's meal on the house. I admire the way you kept things quiet earlier, even though it was clear you were all agitated by the Langfords' behavior."

"We appreciate the kind offer," Momma said as she reached forward with a speed that surprised the innkeeper and pulled the check out of his hands, "but we wouldn't hear of it. We Harts pay what we owe. We always have, and we always will."

Jake nodded. "The Bishops feel that way, too."

"So do the Martins," Phillip joined in.

Mr. Garrett nodded. "I appreciate that. If it's not too much trouble, could I ask you all a favor?"

"Name it and consider it done," I said maybe a little too spontaneously. What had I just promised?

"Would you all be willing to let me bend your ear about my situation? I could use some advice from outsiders, and I admire the four of you and your outlook on life. Maybe some fresh perspective is all that I need. We could all come back to my office now. I won't need more than an hour of your time, and I'd be most appreciative."

It was going to be difficult refusing him in his helpless state, but we were intent on retrieving the Star before anyone else got to it. "Can it wait a few hours?" I asked.

"Certainly," Mr. Garrett said, clearly a little put off by the delay. "May I ask why?"

"We want to drive around in my Jeep and see the town at night," I said, coming up with the only idea I could think of that had the slightest bit of plausibility.

"You want to see Devil's Ridge *at night*?" he asked a bit incredulously. "I love this town, but I've never heard anyone express the least bit of desire to see it in the dark."

"We do it everywhere we go," I lied. "Don't we?"

I needed one member of my party to back me up, but I had my doubts. After all, Jake and Phillip both had an unreasonable fondness for the truth, and my mother had more integrity than I could ever aspire to. To my surprise though, she was the one who answered without even the slightest hesitation. "You'd be amazed by how different things look at night."

Both Jake and Phillip looked at her oddly, but I didn't think that Mr. Garrett even noticed. "Enjoy your drive then, but please, do look me up when you return."

"You can count on it," I said as we all got up and left the table together. I noticed that Phillip and Jake each left a substantial tip for Joy, and I had a hunch that once he saw the size of his gratuity, he'd be emulating his name for days to come.

Once the check was paid, I headed for the parking lot—and, more importantly, my Jeep—when Phillip said, "There's something up in our room that we're going to need."

"I've got us covered," Jake said as he patted his shoulder. It meant that he was carrying a gun with him, not at all an odd occurrence, given the number of bad guys out there who still had a beef with him from his past.

"I do, too, but that wasn't what I was talking about," Phillip said.

Jake shot one eyebrow up quickly and then said, "Lead on, then."

I was about to put my key in the lock of our room when Jake put a hand on mine. "Hold on a second, everyone," he said in a soft voice as he pulled out his revolver.

Phillip followed suit even as he asked, "What is it?"

"I shut a match in the door when we left. Since the Do Not Disturb sign is still on the knob, there's no reason that anyone should have gone into our room." He turned to me and said, "Suzanne, open the door very carefully, and then quickly step to one side. I'm going in hot."

There was no way I was going to talk him out of it, and calling the police was out of the question. Jake, and Phillip as well, *were* the police, in their minds and ours.

It appeared that Mr. Garrett might just have a little more disturbance to deal with that night than he expected.

I turned the key in the lock and then stepped quickly aside, just as Jake had instructed. The speed with which he moved as he flew inside surprised me, and I *knew* what he'd been about to do. Phillip, to his credit, was just half a step behind my husband, his weapon drawn as well.

Momma raised an eyebrow in my direction, but all I could do was shrug.

They were out again in less than a minute, but I swore it felt more like an hour.

"Dot, it's your turn," Phillip said. "Do exactly what Suzanne just did."

I was glad that he hadn't asked me or Jake. After all, Momma was just as much a part of this as the rest of us.

Momma unlocked the door, and again the men went inside quickly with their guns drawn, though I noticed that this time Phillip went in first. Had they worked that out while they'd been in the other room, or had it just been some kind of instinctual cop thing? I had no idea, but I felt safe having them with us.

In less time than before, they came back out together, their guns both holstered. "Whoever was here is long gone," Jake said.

"Were they in *both* rooms?" Momma asked.

"I believe so," Phillip said. "I'm not positive, but I don't think they took anything."

"That's because you had what they wanted with you the entire time," Jake said. "Someone was probably looking for the coded letter in your pocket."

"I'll break Wesley Langford in half," Phillip said angrily as he started back toward the elevator.

"Hang on a second. We can't be sure he did it," Jake told him. "Besides, we don't know what rooms they are in. Do you think Garrett is going to tell you the Langfords' room number when you look as though you're ready to kill someone?"

"Are you saying that we should just let this go?" Phillip asked incredulously.

"No, but we need more proof than we've got right now that Wesley was responsible for this," my husband said calmly. "You had the only thing of value that the thief wanted, so we're still good."

"For now," Phillip said as he went to his bag and pulled out four small flashlights and a six-inch mini crowbar.

"Wow, you really came prepared, didn't you?" I asked him. "What else do you have in that bag?"

"I don't know, but I can attest to the fact that whatever it is, it's heavy," Momma said. "While we're here, I'm going to grab a heavier jacket."

"That's not a bad idea," I said. "We'll meet up again in two minutes."

"Actually, I think we should all stay together for the moment," Jake said.

"Do you really think we're in some kind of danger?" I asked my husband. He was not one to jump at shadows, and it seemed a bit overly cautious to me.

"I don't know, but it's better to be safe than sorry," Jake said.

"That's fine. I'm ready, anyway," Momma said as she grabbed her coat as well as a scarf and a pair of gloves.

"Let's go then," Jake said.

I was about to offer to carry something for Phillip when I noticed that he'd stuffed the lights and the prying tool into the deep pockets of his oversized coat.

It appeared that he was ready for action.

As Jake and Phillip locked their doors behind them, my husband turned to my stepfather. "They had keys for our rooms."

"They did," Phillip agreed.

"Interesting," Jake replied.

"How could you both possibly know that?" Momma asked.

"There were no signs of damage to the locks or the doorframes," I said. "I noticed it earlier."

The men nodded their approval as Momma said, "Sometimes I forget just how good you are at this, Suzanne."

"It's nothing," I said as I noticed Jake closing our door without his telltale match to let us know if someone was inside. "Forgetting something?"

"There's no need now," he said matter-of-factly. "We can expect visitors every time we come back to our room from here on out, so we act accordingly."

Now *I* was getting jumpy.

What had appeared to be a quiet little town had turned out to be much more than we'd bargained for.

Out in the parking lot, instead of heading straight to my Jeep, Jake found a large black SUV parked in one corner away from everyone else.

"Is that the same vehicle that followed us?" I asked him. "If it is, then Wesley and Nicole were telling the truth about driving something else here."

"Possibly," Jake said. He studied the vehicle from the outside and even tried the doors with his hand wrapped up in his jacket sleeve, but it was locked.

"What do you make of that being here now?" Phillip asked him.

"I'm not sure. Right now, it's just one more piece of information. What do you all say to us taking that little drive now?"

"I'm all for it," I said, and as Momma and Phillip nodded in agreement as well, we got into my Jeep and headed to the old library site, and quite possibly the treasure that had brought us all there in the first place.

Chapter 10

"TURN HERE, SUZANNE!" Jake barked at me suddenly.

Even as I was doing as he said, I protested, "But we're nowhere near the old library."

"I know, but I have a feeling that someone's following us."

Phillip and Momma craned their necks around, and I looked in my rearview mirror to see if I could see what he was talking about. "I don't see anybody back there. In fact, there haven't been any headlights since we left the inn," I told him.

"Somebody's running dark without their lights on," Jake said. "Make a left here," he said as a side street came up.

I wasn't about to disagree with him. I might have yanked the wheel a little too abruptly in my enthusiasm to make the turn.

"You have passengers in the backseat, Suzanne. Please don't forget that," Momma said.

"Sorry," I said.

"No, it's my fault," Jake said. "I'm probably just jumping at shadows again. The truth is that I've been on edge ever since we left April Springs," he admitted.

Phillip put a hand on my husband's shoulder. "I've been a little spooked myself, but that being said, I'll take your gut feeling over anyone else's in the world."

"What if I'm wrong, though?" Jake asked with a slight smile.

"Look at it this way," Phillip said. "It can't hurt anything taking a little evasive action every now and then."

"Unless it means that I'm losing my touch, my edge," Jake said so softly that I doubted anyone in back had even heard it.

I reached over and patted his knee. I wanted to reassure him that he was as sharp as ever, at least as far as I was concerned, but I seriously doubted that he'd said it asking for sympathy. Anyway, the pat must have worked, because he glanced over at me and smiled ever so briefly. I loved having an unspoken language with this man, and I looked forward to the opportunity to keep developing it for many years to come.

On a whim, I took another side street without being told to.

It turned out that it was twenty feet from a dead end.

"We've got 'em cornered now," I said, laughing, as I started to put the Jeep into Reverse.

"Actually, that's not a bad idea," Jake said. "Once you've turned around so you're facing the other way, turn off your lights and shut off the engine."

I did as I was told, and then I asked him facetiously, "Should we duck down, too?"

"Not unless we see someone else coming," Jake said in all seriousness.

"I was kidding," I said, finding myself whispering for no apparent reason.

"I wasn't," Jake replied.

After five minutes of silence, Momma asked, "I don't mean to complain, but it's getting cold back here. How long do we just sit and wait?"

Jake shrugged. "That's probably long enough. Oh, well. It was worth a shot. Let's go, Suzanne."

"Just because we didn't see anyone doesn't mean that someone *wasn't* following us," I told him as I started the engine again. "We could have lost them because of your expert tactics in stealth."

"Oh, yes, I'm a regular ninja," Jake said, trying to force a grin.

"Should we go get the Star now?" Phillip asked eagerly.

"Yes, but I'd like to take one more precaution, if you all don't mind," Jake said.

"Name it," I said, curious as to what else he had up his sleeve.

"Park on Winston, not Perkins," he requested. "Go down about a hundred yards and then find a place to pull over."

"Any particular reason why?" Momma asked him.

"I don't want to announce our presence near the old library if I can help it," Jake said. "Unless I miss my guess, we should be able to cut through someone's yard and get exactly where we need to be without anyone even knowing that we're there."

"Don't get me wrong. I like your plan, but the flashlight beams might give us away," I said as I parked the Jeep as requested and got out. It was definitely getting colder out now.

At least we weren't getting freezing rain, or even snow, for that matter.

I guessed that was something.

In all honesty, I didn't like being cold or wet, but I *hated* being both at the same time.

"I've got the lenses mostly taped off," Phillip said. "Turn yours on and see."

I did as he instructed, and I found that the beam of light had been lessened considerably. "Are we going to have enough light to even see with these things?"

"Our eyes will get used to the amount of light soon enough," Jake said. "Come on, let's go."

"Watch out for the swing set," I said as one of the supports caught my ankle and sent me sprawling to the hard ground below.

"Are you okay?" Jake asked me as he helped me up.

"I'm fine, if you don't count my dignity, my grace, or my general self-esteem," I said as I bent over and retrieved my flashlight.

"Suzanne, you really should be more careful," Momma said. I knew that she hadn't meant to sound as though she was scolding me, but that was the way it came out, at least to my ears.

Instead of barking back at her, I simply said, "Thanks for the tip. I'll be sure to work on that."

Momma must have known that her comment had dug into my already sore feelings. "I'm sorry, Suzanne. I know you're a grown woman, but sometimes I can't seem to help myself."

"I think it's great you two are so close," Phillip said, "but could we please go get the Star and talk about all of this later?"

He was about to jump out of his skin with anticipation, and we all knew it.

"Of course," Momma said. "You and Jake lead on."

We got to the brick wall without any more incidents. The night was dark, and I could see my breath billowing out in the muted light of the flashlight beam. Phillip started at the missing lion and then he started counting.

Unfortunately, the brick we needed to be loose was tight.

"Did someone remortar it?" Jake asked as he used his own light to help illuminate the brick in question.

"No, it's just wedged in there with something," Phillip said as he began working the thin tapered end of his small crowbar into the crevices around the brick in question, finally starting to work it loose.

"I can take a stab at it, if you'd like," Jake offered, but Phillip brushed the offer off.

"I've almost got it." He shoved the crowbar in the joint a bit harder, and the brick popped out as though it had been on springs.

Taking his light and peering into the cavity, Phillip sighed and then said heavily, his voice barely hiding his massive disappointment, "It's not here."

I knew that it would be a tight fit jamming that gold relic into the narrow opening, but I figured maybe some of the building material had been hollowed out to allow enough room for the Star to safely sit.

"Hang on a second," Jake said as he moved closer to the opening.

At that moment, I heard a car door close on the road. It had clearly meant to be done in silence, but the door must have slipped out of the person's hand, and there was enough sound for us to know that someone had managed to follow us after all.

"Let's get out of here," Phillip said even as Jake was jamming the loose brick back into place. "Hurry."

We followed him back through the other yard in the darkness, and my hand was on the door of my Jeep when I heard a gunshot behind us.

Clearly someone was done playing around.

"Go, Suzanne!" Jake shouted.

I tore out of there without even looking back the second I knew that my family was all safe inside.

"I can't believe you two didn't shoot back," I said as I drove hurriedly back to the inn.

"It was dark, we didn't have a clear target in sight, and you two were with us," Jake said, ticking the reasons off on his fingers as he spoke.

"To be honest with you, I thought about doing it anyway," Phillip admitted guiltily.

"So did I," Jake said with a shrug, "but what counts is that we didn't."

"It's a shame about your coded letter clue not working out," Momma told her husband as we neared the inn. "I know how much you were counting on finding the Star."

"It's okay," Phillip said. "I've run into dead ends before, and I'm sure it will happen again."

"Don't count us out just yet," Jake said.

"Why not?" I asked him.

"Let's wait until we're inside one of our rooms and I'll tell you," he said as we piled out of the Jeep and hurried inside.

"Hang on a second," Jake said before we left the parking lot. "Notice anything different?"

"The black SUV is gone," Phillip said quickly.

"So then you noticed it, too," Jake replied, clearly a little deflated that he hadn't been the only one who'd spotted the vehicle's absence.

"No, not until you mentioned it," Phillip said with a grin. "You've still got it, buddy."

"I hope you're right," Jake said, but it was clear he was relieved to get the small victory.

"Nicole and Wesley's car is still gone, too," I said.

"What does that signify?" Momma asked.

"It could have been either group that took a shot at us back at the old library," I told her.

"Or someone else completely," Jake added.

"Do you really think there are other people after the Star, too?" I asked him.

"Suzanne, that thing is priceless, especially if you ignore the offered reward and keep it all for yourself. I imagine there are any number of people who would love to find it, including most of the residents of Devil's Ridge."

"I never looked at it that way," I said, suddenly wondering exactly who in town I could or could not trust now.

It wasn't a particularly good feeling.

"Don't worry, we'll keep our eyes and ears open," Jake said as we hurried inside the building to get out of the cold and to figure out what our next move was going to be.

I couldn't wait to get up to our room to find out what Jake had been talking about, but apparently I was going to have to delay finding out for the moment despite my wishes.

I hated when I was thwarted like that.

Jimmy Garrett was standing at the door to his office, and he'd clearly been waiting for us ever since we'd left the Overlook Inn.

It appeared that we were going to have to hear the innkeeper out before I was going to get a chance to learn what was on my husband's mind.

"Are you sure you have the time to listen to my woes?" Jimmy Garrett said as we approached him.

"Of course," Momma said, and then she looked around. There were a few guests enjoying the fire in the lobby, and they could easily hear everything we were about to say. "Is there someplace a little more private we might go?"

"My office is right behind me," Jimmy said as he turned and led us into a nice space tucked away behind the front desk.

"Wow, this is much nicer than I expected," I said as we followed him into a rather generous space. There were bookcases there, a nice large quarter-sawn oak desk, two couches, a few chairs, and even a small stone fireplace that mimicked the one out front.

"What can I say? The original owner liked nice things," Jimmy said as he took his seat behind his desk. "Actually, that was what got him into trouble. He insisted on only the best of everything, and when the guests didn't come in the droves he'd been hoping for, he couldn't sustain the place. I know exactly what happened to him. I bought the inn at a steep discount, and given my troubles, especially lately, I haven't even been able to make my payments on time as it is."

"Tell us what troubles you've been having," Jake said as he settled onto one of the couches. I took the seat beside him as Momma and Phillip sat in free chairs, and we all listened to what the innkeeper had to say.

"Where to begin is the question," Garrett mused. "I suppose it all started a week after I signed the paperwork to buy the inn."

"Was anyone else interested in the property?" Momma asked him.

"There were a few groups, from what I heard, but the bids were sealed, so no one but the bank really knew. To be honest with you, I was a bit surprised that I got it."

"Go on," Phillip told him.

"The problems began almost immediately. At first, it was just a few guests complaining about odd noises in the middle of the night, things being moved around, that kind of thing. I assumed it was mostly due to overactive imaginations, and I had a word with the housekeeping staff not to disturb something unless it was totally necessary for cleaning purposes. I hoped that would take care of it, but then things started to escalate."

"How so?" Momma asked. I considered myself a good listener, but she was amazing at it. It wasn't her words so much as it was the complete and utter interest she showed in everything Mr. Garrett told us. For that moment, she focused one hundred percent of her attention on him, as though he was the most vital and interesting thing in the universe. It was heady stuff; there was no doubt about it.

"Our computer system started acting up, losing some reservations and double billing others. Then food started going bad mysteriously in the kitchen, and I started having a hard time keeping staff on. It was as though no one wanted to work here. I paid fair wages, and there weren't a lot of other jobs to be had in the region, but people kept leaving."

"Did they say why?" Jake asked.

"The only thing most of them would say was that they got a bad vibe from the place," the innkeeper said with a shrug. "I know the inn has had a bit of a reputation for being haunted, but it was mostly all a joke in the past because of the coincidence of that blasted hotel in the King novel. Then I started to wonder if maybe everyone was right."

"So, something happened directly to you. What was it that made you change your mind?"

"I started finding doors open that should have been locked, windows that I knew were shut standing wide open, papers being moved, though not by me, whispers when there was no one around, things like that," he admitted. "I don't know why I'm bothering you all with this. You can't exactly get rid of my ghosts any more than I can."

"I wouldn't be so sure about that," Jake said without the slightest of smiles.

Chapter 11

"YOU'RE PULLING MY LEG, aren't you?" Mr. Garrett asked, clearly not daring to hope that my husband might be serious.

"Jake rarely kids about things like this," I said.

"Then tell me. I'll do anything."

"Mr. Garrett, I have a question for you first. Is there any way you can find out who else was bidding on the inn when you bought it?" Momma asked. Clearly she and Jake were on the same page. It may have taken me a bit longer to get there, but then I got it at about the same time that Phillip did.

"We know one thing. At least one current employee was bidding, or they've been hired by someone who was," I said.

Mr. Garrett looked puzzled by my statement. "Why do you say that?"

"I'm sure that you'd see it, too, if you weren't so close to it," I told him. "Everything points to someone on the inside tampering with your operation, and there's nothing otherworldly about that. Someone wants you out, and the fact that they're ramping up their antics means that they are getting impatient."

"But why would someone else *want* a dying business?" he asked. "Especially now that a developer is building another hotel in town? It makes this place even more worthless than it was before."

"But has ground been officially broken on the new structure?" Momma asked.

"No, but the dozers are coming in a few days," Garrett insisted. "Everybody in town knows that."

"Have you *personally* seen them? Or the building permit, for that matter? Surely there need to be plans on file at the city planners office if something of that magnitude is about to happen," Momma explained.

"The problem is that he can't check it out now," Phillip said. "Nobody will be there."

"Not necessarily," Mr. Garrett said. "My cousin's husband works at the planning and permitting office, and he's got a key to the place. If I ask her, she'll get him to go check it out right now." He made a quick call and then hung up with a grin. "He was watching a game on TV, but she said he'll do it right now and call me back anyway. They only live four minutes from his office, so we'll have our answer in no time."

"Excellent. While you are waiting to hear back from him, if I were you, I'd make a list of all of your current employees, including your absentee night desk manager," I said.

"Do you honestly think someone is doing this who works here?" he asked. I was certain the prospect made him equal parts angry and sad. After all, nobody likes being betrayed by those around him.

"It's a sure thing," Jake said. "Nothing that has been happening could have been done by an outsider. When you think about it, it all makes sense, especially if you find out that no one is building anything at the old library site after all."

"How did you know that was where the hotel was going to be built?" he looked at Jake curiously.

"We ran into Leslie Ann, your librarian, and she mentioned it," I said, covering for my husband quickly.

"Yes, Leslie Ann has been a sympathetic shoulder for me to cry on ever since I made the mistake of buying the Overlook," he said.

"She told us that you two dated a while ago," I said, curious to hear his side of the story and learn what had really happened between them.

The innkeeper blushed slightly before he answered. "We went out a few times in high school, but then she dumped me for a college guy. After that fizzled out, she tried to start things up again with me a few times, but my feelings were shattered the first time, and I didn't want to risk getting dumped again."

"Maybe finding love is worth the risk of a little pain," I said.

He shrugged. "I'm not sure she'd even want to start dating me again now that my life is such a mess."

"But we're working on fixing that right now, aren't we?" I asked him.

"Suzanne, don't push the man into doing something he is clearly uncomfortable doing," Momma scolded me. "You and your matchmaking attempts are often over the line."

I was about to apologize when Mr. Garrett surprised me. "Actually, she's right, ma'am. If we get this mess figured out and my inn is safe, I'll ask Leslie Ann out again, no matter what might happen in the end."

"Then let's figure this out," I said with enthusiasm. Maybe Momma was right. Sometimes I did cross a line or two, but I enjoyed seeing folks find each other. After all, if I hadn't found Jake, I knew that my life would have been much the poorer because of it. It was just fine being alone, but it could be so much better with someone you cared about.

At least that was how I felt about it.

"I still can't imagine someone who works here doing this," Mr. Garrett said.

"I know it's difficult for you, but everything points to it," Phillip said as the innkeeper's phone rang.

"That was quick," I said.

"What can I say? My cousin is an excellent motivator," he said with a slight smile as he answered the phone. "Sorry. Yes. Yes." There was a longer pause and then, "Are you sure? Okay, thanks. I appreciate it. Good-bye." As Mr. Garrett ended the call, he looked baffled. "You were right. No permits have been filed for demolition or construction of any kind anywhere near the old library."

"I'm curious about something else. Where did you first hear the rumor about another hotel being built in town?" I asked him. Maybe, if we got lucky, we could trace it back to the source.

"It was at the DINE," he said. "A few old men who are notorious gossips were spreading the word around at breakfast one day about a month ago, and by lunchtime everyone in town had heard the news."

"Are you talking about the Liar's Club?" I asked him. I'd actually seen them holding court at their table earlier that day when I'd been at the DINE.

"Yes, those are the two I'm talking about. I'm afraid it would be impossible to track the origin of the story down. Even if they remembered who told them about the new hotel, neither man would have the slightest inclination to tell me the truth. They haven't been fans of mine for several years."

Jake asked, "Would *they* have any reason to help someone shut you down?"

"I wouldn't have said so before tonight, but it's possible." He paused a moment and then added softly, "There is something odd about that, though."

"What's that?" Phillip asked.

"One of the men happens to be Joy's brother-in-law."

"It's got to all be one big coincidence," Mr. Garrett continued. "Joy would *never* try to run me off."

"I know it's hard to imagine," I said. "I liked him from the first moment we met, but he's an employee here, so he's bound to have access to keys from time to time. Would he have the capital to mount a bid for the inn?"

"Not alone, but if the three of them pooled their resources, they might be able to swing it," Mr. Garrett said. "I'm going to go have to have a little chat with my favorite employee after you all go back upstairs."

"Why don't you bring him in here now, with us all here?" Jake suggested.

"Are you going to help me interrogate him?" the innkeeper asked, clearly pleased that he wouldn't have to ask the older man the tough questions that needed to be asked.

"We won't say a word if you don't want us to," Jake said, looking at me until I nodded my agreement. "It will have quite a bit of power alone if there are witnesses, and if you want us to chime in, all you have to do is ask."

"That sounds like the best way to handle it. We might as well go ahead and get it over with," Mr. Garrett said.

Jake cautioned him, "Don't tell him we are in here, and don't worry about what you're going to say. You are just asking questions, so don't lose sight of that. He may or may not be innocent, so don't say anything you can't take back later. Right now, you're just looking for information."

"That's easy for you to say, but I'm not a detective," Mr. Garrett said.

"Jake, maybe you and Phillip should handle the questioning," I suggested softly. "You both have a great deal of experience with this kind of thing." I turned to the innkeeper and explained, "They happen to both be former police chiefs for April Springs, North Carolina."

"Would you handle it for me? That would be great," Mr. Garrett said, the relief clearly flooding through him. "I know I'll blow it if it's left up to me."

"I agree that a professional should do it, but Jake should do it alone," Phillip countered.

Momma quickly rose to his defense. "Phillip Martin, you are just as able and qualified to participate in this as Jake is, and you know it."

My stepfather reached over and patted Momma's hand. "You don't have to bolster my confidence, Dot. I just don't want Joy to feel as though we are ganging up on him. It would be better if Jake handled the questions alone."

"If you're sure," Jake said. "I don't mind, so you can do the solo interrogation, if you'd like."

"Thanks, but if it's all the same to you, I'd like to sit back and take notes while I watch how a former state police investigator goes about it," Phillip said with a grin.

Mr. Garrett looked a bit bewildered by our revelations. "I never thought to inquire, but I'm asking you now. Exactly who are you people, and why are you staying at my inn?"

"Haven't you heard? We're on business and vacation," I said with a grin, giving him the same answer we'd inadvertently given him earlier. "Don't worry about it, and think of it as your lucky day. Now go get Joy."

While he was gone, I looked over at Jake. I wanted to ask him what he'd been about to tell us when we'd first arrived back at the Overlook, but it was clear that he was putting on his game face, no doubt thinking about the questions he wanted to ask Joy and the order he would ask his queries in. I knew better than to disturb that particular process, so I looked around the expansive office while I waited. My office at the donut shop was a hole compared to this place. Even my eating area wasn't as nice as the private space we were in at the moment.

It was good enough for me, though.

Donut Hearts suited me just fine in just about every way imaginable.

While we waited, Momma said, "Oh, by the way, I forgot to tell you, Suzanne. I heard from Gabby Williams just before we left."

Gabby used to run a gently used upscale clothing shop right beside my business, at least she did until a lunatic decided to burn it to the ground, preferably with her in it. Her business had been a total loss, and she'd taken the insurance money and immediately left town. Most folks around April Springs believed that the irritating woman was gone for good, but I hoped not. We'd developed an odd friendship over the years, and I'd found myself missing her, much to my own surprise. "How's she doing?"

"She's coming back to April Springs," Momma said. "Evidently retirement is boring her."

"Is she opening another shop?" I asked.

"She wouldn't say, but she did ask me if I had any empty buildings in town that might be for sale or lease," Momma said.

I felt a twinge of disappointment at the news. "I kind of hoped she'd rebuild ReNEWed beside me," I said.

"Then be careful what you wish for, because she asked me for the names of some good contractors as well," Momma answered.

I was about to ask more when Mr. Garrett came back into his office, looking distinctly puzzled.

I looked behind him. "Where's Joy?"

"Apparently the moment he saw us come into the office, he left in the middle of his shift," Mr. Garrett said.

"Well then, there's your answer," Momma said.

"Not so fast," Phillip interjected. "It may be a coincidence."

"I doubt that," Momma said.

I decided it was time to speak up. "Did anyone else notice him lose control of our tray of drinks as he approached our table earlier?"

"I did. Why, is that significant?" Momma asked me.

"Maybe not, but it was exactly when Jake admitted to being a former state police investigator," I said, not liking the idea that I was adding to the case against the good-natured server.

"I didn't see it, but then again, you two were the only ones facing him," Jake said. "I'm sure what you saw was accurate though, as well as being rather telling."

"Either way, I'll speak to him when he comes in tomorrow, with or without you," Mr. Garrett said with a sigh.

"*If* he comes in," I replied.

"If indeed," he echoed. "Well, I've taken up enough of your time tonight. I appreciate it more than I can tell you."

"We're happy to help," I said. I hated the thought of that cool old guy who'd served us being a bad guy, but I'd known some nice folks in the past who had committed murder, so it wasn't a stretch thinking that the charming server was a part of the scheme to get rid of Mr. Garrett.

"If you need us, at least for tonight, you know where to find us," Phillip said as he shook the innkeeper's hand.

After we said our good nights, we headed upstairs.

Momma and Phillip were about to go to their room when Jake said softly, "Hang on a second. You both need to come with us."

"What's going on?" Phillip asked.

"There's something I need to show you," Jake answered, and that was all that he would say.

Chapter 12

"WHERE DID YOU GET THAT?" Phillip asked eagerly as Jake showed us the torn and faded piece of paper.

"It was stuck in the bottom of the hole of the brick wall at the library," he admitted.

"I never saw it," Phillip said in wonder.

"That's probably because you were expecting to find the Southern Shooting Star," Jake said.

"So were you," he countered.

"To be fair, I had a little more time than you did," my husband said, trying to dismiss Phillip's comment. Not to take anything away from my stepfather's prowess as an investigator, Jake was the cream of a very rich crop.

"What does it say?" Momma asked.

"First, I want Phillip to tell us if it's really from Tommy Malone," Jake said as he handed over the paper.

"It's his handwriting," Phillip said excitedly.

"How can you be so sure so quickly?" Momma asked and then hurriedly added, "Not that I doubt you."

"Dot, I've studied the man's handwriting enough over the past few months to authenticate it without a shadow of a doubt."

I looked over at the paper and read it aloud.

"Had to move the cursed thing again. COPS on my tail. UNDER DR101."

"Does anyone know what it means?" I asked them.

"I don't have a clue," Jake admitted. "I was hoping Phillip might know."

He just shook his head as he continued to stare at the brittle and faded piece of paper. "Sorry, it doesn't mean a thing to me."

"So we're up against another dead end," I said as I snapped a photo of the note with my phone. I figured it wouldn't hurt to have a record of it with me, even if I had no clue as to what it might mean.

"I'm afraid that it's the mother of all dead ends," Phillip said as he slumped down into a nearby chair. "If we don't have a clue what it means, we don't have any hope of ever finding the Southern Shooting Star."

"What could *UNDER DR1O1* even mean? Under a driveway? Under a dryer?" I asked. "And what does the 101 signify?"

"Are we even sure those are ones?" Jake asked. "They could just as easily be 'I's."

"Is that really any more helpful?" Momma asked. "DR1O1 makes a bit more sense than DRIOI. I think he was interrupted by someone before he could finish what he'd been trying to write."

"Maybe so," Jake said.

"Then where does that leave us? I was really hoping your Star would be there, Phillip," Jake said as he patted my stepfather on the back.

"So did I," Phillip said with a sigh. "Well, at least we tried."

Momma frowned at all three of us. "We're not really just giving up, are we?"

"I know it's not in your nature," I told her. "It's not in mine, either, but unless we can decipher what the code means, there's not much we can do about it."

"Phillip, were there *any* references to DR1O1 in the letters you read?"

"See for yourself," he said as he brought out a few more documents from his large pockets.

"I thought you had just the letter with the code in it," I told him.

"Nope. That's all I showed you, but I've been keeping a few of the more critical letters with me since we left April Springs."

"That's a good thing," I said as I took one of the letters from him. After scanning it quickly, I said, "There aren't any '1's or '0's to compare this to," I said.

"No, or capital 'O's, either," Phillip commented. "There are a pair of 'I's, though. What do you think?"

"He clearly wrote the note in the wall in a hurry," Jake said with a frown. "I can't tell what he really meant to write."

"I can't, either," Phillip agreed, the resignation thick in his voice. "Oh, well. Easy come, easy go. It looks like I dragged us all here on a wild goose chase."

"Are you kidding? It's been an adventure," I said, trying to buoy his spirits. "Besides, it's been fun hanging out with the two of you, no matter what we have or have not found. Right, Jake?"

"You bet," he said. "Don't forget, we've helped Jimmy Garrett, too, so it wasn't a complete waste of our time. Plus, it's not every day you get shot at. In my book, that means that we were at least doing something right."

"There's always that," Phillip said. "So, do we leave first thing in the morning and head back to April Springs?"

"What about your truck, Phillip?" Momma reminded him.

He grinned. "Funny, but for a second there, I'd forgotten all about that."

"I don't know about the rest of you, but I wanted to hang around until late afternoon, anyway," I said. "After all, there's no real rush to get back home, and this area really is beautiful. What do you say?"

"I say we do it," Jake agreed. "How about it, Dot?"

"I'm always ready to spend time with you both," she said. Nudging her husband with her knee, she asked, "What do you think, Phillip?"

"Why not?" he finally asked with a grin.

"Should we at least cancel our breakfast tomorrow with the deputy sheriff?" Jake asked.

"If it's all the same to you, I'd like to go ahead and meet with him," Phillip said and then turned to us. "That is, only if you ladies don't mind."

"Momma and I can go down to the DINE and have breakfast," I said happily.

"I like that plan," she said with a slight smile. It would be fun having breakfast, just the two of us. I loved the time we spent with the men in our lives, but there was nothing quite like our mother–daughter occasions, no matter where we were.

I stifled a yawn. "What should we do with the rest of our evening?" I asked.

"How much of it do you think we have left?" Jake asked me with a grin.

"Me? I'm not sleepy," I said as my yawn proved me to be a liar.

"Honestly, the trip and all of this excitement has worn me out as well," Momma said. "Shall we call it a night, Phillip?"

"Sure," he said, and then he looked at the note again. "Mind if I keep this?"

"I don't mind at all," Jake said.

"Don't forget your letters, too," I offered.

After Phillip gathered everything up and put it all carefully away in his pocket, he said, "I don't care if it didn't lead us to the Star, that was good detective work finding that note in the first place, Jake."

"Thank you, sir. Coming from you, that's a real compliment."

Once they were gone, I kissed my husband soundly.

"What was that for? Not that I'm complaining," Jake said.

"You could have held finding that note over Phillip's head, but you were really gracious about it."

"I meant what I said, Suzanne. That's one of the reasons cops like to work in teams. One might pick up on something the other misses. It's just too bad that it didn't pan out this time."

"That's life though, isn't it? These things happen," I said.

"They do indeed," he answered.

As I drifted off to sleep a little later, I couldn't help thinking about the Southern Shooting Star, wondering where it was tonight. It would have been wonderful finding it, but I was sure that it would have come with its own set of complications. Something that valuable would be dangerous to have in your possession, and people had been known to do bad things for a lot less.

All in all, not recovering the artifact was probably for the best.

At least we'd have a neat story to tell about once *almost* finding such a well-known piece of history.

"Are you ready for breakfast?" I asked Momma the next morning. The men were already in the dining room of the inn, waiting for the deputy sheriff to show up.

"I'm absolutely starving," Momma said. "The mountain air always gives me an appetite."

My definition of being hungry and my mother's were completely different. Her idea of gorging was eating an entire single waffle, whereas I didn't mind ordering an extra to go along with the two or three I liked to start with. Then again, she was just about small enough to put in someone's front pocket, unlike her big-boned daughter.

Right, that was why my clothes were stretched almost to the limit.

I had big bones.

"Let's go, then."

We drove over in my Jeep, and we were just parking when I noticed two men coming out of the DINE. One was large and meaty, with hands that looked as though they were designed to tear things apart. He had a crew cut, and his bulky jacket only hinted at the muscles underneath. His companion, a thin young man with the oddest blue hair, looked overwhelmed in every single aspect of their relationship. "I want to go home, Mr. Duncan," the blue-haired man protested.

"Until I get what I came for, that's just too bad," the beefy man answered as I pulled Momma back so we could eavesdrop without being easily seen. "Now get in the car and keep your mouth shut, Henry. If I want your opinion about something, I'll beat it out of you."

I thought it was just an expression, but from the pale look on the slender man's face, I wondered if it might not be rooted in the truth after all.

Both car doors opened, and the men climbed inside and drove away without even noticing us. To be fair, I had parked my Jeep between two monster trucks, so we were hard to spot.

"What was that all about?" I asked Momma.

"I don't know, but I fear for the safety of the slimmer man."

"Should we call someone?" I asked her.

"Who exactly would we call, Suzanne, and what would we say, assuming that we managed to figure out the first part?" Momma asked me.

"That's a pair of fair points. You noticed the kind of vehicle they were in, didn't you?"

"It was a dark SUV of some kind," Momma replied.

"As a matter of fact, it was black, and unless I miss my guess, it's the same car that followed us up the mountain *and* was parked at the inn last night," I told her. "Did you happen to see the license plate?"

"They drove past us so quickly that I missed it," Momma admitted.

"Don't feel bad. I missed it, too," I answered. I started to call Jake, but then I thought better of it. It could wait until after his breakfast with the deputy sheriff, and besides, since the Star was impossible to find, the fact that someone had followed us to Devil's Ridge wasn't quite as dire as it had seemed the day before. "Let's eat, shall we?"

"That sounds like an excellent plan to me," Momma said.

We found a table, and my favorite server approached us quickly. Of course, Eleanora was the *only* server I'd met there, but still, I liked her. On our way over to our spot, I had noticed that the two older men were back at their table under the Liar's Club sign. Now that I knew a bit of their history, I thought them quite a bit less quaint than I had the day before. If they were conspiring to drive Jimmy Garrett out of the innkeeping business, then they were definitely on my bad list.

"Back again so soon?" Eleanora asked with a grin. "Either we're growing on you, or there's no other place in town to have breakfast besides the Overlook, at least while it's still there."

"Do you really think it's going to shut down?" I asked her as I took the offered menu from her.

Lowering her voice, she pointed to the Liar's Club table and said, "If it were up to them, it would."

"Why do they dislike Jimmy Garrett so much?" I asked.

"Who knows? Around here, it could be a blood feud that's been going on for four or five generations," she said. "Some folks just seem to like holding a grudge."

I couldn't tell if she was kidding or not, and the truth was, I wasn't even sure that I *wanted* to know. "What's good on the breakfast menu?"

"Our pancakes are the best in Virginia, at least according to me," Eleanora said with a grin. "The oatmeal's okay, the eggs are the same as you'd get anywhere, but don't order the scramble. It's whatever they have in back that didn't sell the day before mixed in with some powdered eggs, and I wouldn't serve it to a hungry dog."

I'd run into more honest servers in this town than in all of North Carolina. What was it about these folks? Did they really not care about the impression they gave to strangers? In a way, I liked it, though. I never trusted anyone who thought that *everything* they served was good. There were donuts I wouldn't offer for sale, or even give away, when the recipe went awry, and I wasn't afraid who knew it.

"I'll have the pancakes," I said. "How many per order?"

"One for the regular, two for the super. I'll put you down for one," Eleanora said as she jotted my order down on her pad.

"I don't know. I'm kind of hungry. I think I can handle two," I protested.

"Hang on a second," she said with an odd grin as she left our table and headed into the kitchen.

"What just happened? Did I somehow offend her?" I asked Momma softly.

"I don't see how," she replied. "Maybe you should just get one, Suzanne. After all, we'll be eating again in three or four hours, so one pancake should hold you."

"I guess so," I said, though I wasn't crazy about anyone practicing portion control with my food intake, especially when I was on vacation.

Eleanora came out with a massive pancake covering the edges of a huge plate. "This isn't for you, so don't get excited, but I wanted you to see what one pancake looked like." Her grin was infectious.

"You know what? One sounds good to me after all," I said.

Momma looked troubled. "Is there a smaller size, perhaps?"

"We offer one on the senior menu, but I don't think you qualify. You have to be over sixty," Eleanora told her with a grin. "If you order that, I'm afraid I'm going to have to see some ID first."

Momma laughed. "Don't worry, your healthy tip has already been ensured," she answered. "I'll have the smaller senior version, with sausage and coffee, please."

"How about you?" she asked me.

"Bacon, and how about some orange juice to go with it? I feel like a real buckaroo this morning."

"Well, yeehaw, then," she said with a laugh and left to place our orders.

I had my doubts that I'd even be able to make a dent in my single massive pancake, but if it was as good as Eleanor promised, I'd give it my best shot.

As Eleanora returned with our food, I asked, "Did you happen to see a skinny guy with blue hair arguing with his breakfast companion this morning?"

"Oh, yes," she said as she set our plates down. "The big guy polished off a super pancake order. I was worried for a second there that he was going to eat the plate, too. Not many folks, men or women, even try it, but he made it look easy. I didn't like the way he looked at me, though," she said with a bit of a shiver at the end.

"Really? Was there anything specific you could put your finger on?" Momma asked her.

"I couldn't name it at first, but as soon as they left, I finally figured it out. I felt as though I was one of those sausage links on your plate right now hanging in a store window, and he was deciding whether he wanted me or not. I hated it."

The chilling way she'd described the experience gave me goose bumps, and I hadn't even been there to witness it. "Does that happen a lot?"

She shrugged. "I'm no beauty queen, but I get my share of admirers in here. A lot of the men who eat at the DINE are harmless flirts, but there was nothing harmless about that guy. I don't mind telling you that I almost cheered when he left with his pal."

"How did the blue-haired man strike you?" I asked her.

"Like he was afraid to breathe for fear of offending the brute," she said softly. The bell in the kitchen rang, and she added quickly, "I've got to take care of that."

"What do you think?" I asked Momma as soon as Eleanora was gone.

"I think that you are going to have a difficult time eating that pancake," she said as she gestured to my plate.

"I'm talking about what Eleanora just told us," I insisted.

"I know that, but I don't want to think about it right now. I just want to enjoy breakfast with my daughter without considering how many truly bad people there are in the world."

"I'd like that, too," I said. After that, I tried to keep the conversation light, but there was a pall over us, whether it was because of the unfulfilled quest, the bully we'd seen earlier, or simply the town in general.

On our way out, after paying and leaving Eleanor a hefty tip, I lingered at the Liar's Club table for a moment. "We know what you're up to," I told them seriously.

"What are you talking about?" one of them said, clearly caught off guard by my blunt statement.

"Haven't you heard? Joy told Jimmy everything, and then he took off and headed for the hills."

"Who *are* you?" the other man asked me, his face as white as snow.

"Me? I'm nobody," I answered. "At least I'm not the person you should be worried about."

"Are you coming?" Momma asked me as she drifted back in my direction.

"I am," I said, and then I turned back to them with my brightest smile. "Have a good day, gentlemen. If I were you, I'd enjoy it. After all, you never know what tomorrow might bring."

"Did you just threaten those men back there, Suzanne?" Momma asked me once we were out in the parking lot.

"No, ma'am. Everything I said to them was perfectly cordial."

She shook her head. "One of these days, you're going to antagonize the wrong person. You know that, don't you?"

"If you think about it, I already have, and on more than one occasion, to boot," I said, remembering when I'd faced murderers down in the past. Standing up to a couple of weasels sitting at the Liar's Club table didn't seem all that scary to me, but then again, as the people closest to me often commented on, I'd changed over the years since I'd started investigating murder. It had made me a little harder, a little bolder, but a lot more loving to the people I truly cared about. After all, I knew better than most how fleeting life could be, and I was determined to make sure that everyone I loved knew it.

Given that fact, if I had it all to do over again, I wouldn't change a thing.

The truth was, I liked the strong, independent, and yes, sometimes stubborn woman I'd grown into over the years.

As we walked to my Jeep, I felt my feet start to slide out from under me. Momma steadied me just in time, keeping me from wiping out in the parking lot. "I didn't even see a slick spot on the pavement," I said once I'd recovered completely.

"Black ice can be deadly," Momma said. "I've fallen on it myself in the past. The pavement might look wet, but it's actually ice." She looked up at the sky, and I did as well. A few fat flakes began to tumble down toward us.

"It's snowing," I said, holding out my hand as a few flakes landed and then promptly melted.

"I hope it doesn't interfere with our trip home," Momma said.

"I wouldn't mind getting snowed in up here for another day or two," I told her. "After all, we've got a restaurant, a fireplace in the lobby, and a warm place to sleep at night. I can think of a lot worse places to be stranded in."

"So can I, but I'd still like to go home today," Momma said as we got into my Jeep and started back to the inn.

"What's up?" I asked her. "Is something wrong?"

"No, nothing in particular. Just call it a feeling."

"What kind of feeling?" I asked her. My mother was not generally known for having premonitions, at least not as far as I knew.

"A bad one," was all that she would say, and we drove the rest of the way back to the inn in silence.

Chapter 13

"ARE THEY HONESTLY *still* having breakfast?" Momma asked me as we both peeked into the restaurant at the Overlook. "What on earth do they have to talk about?"

"Come on, three cops? You're kidding, right? If we're lucky, we'll get out of here by the time the truck gets here at noon. That's checkout time, right?"

"It is, though I feel that after last night, Mr. Garrett will allow us a little leeway in when we leave the inn."

"What do you think about that situation?" I asked her softly.

"What do you mean?"

"Can you believe those three men, one a long-time trusted employee, would try to sabotage his life, all for a hotel?" I asked.

"Suzanne, I've seen much worse done for far less," she said. "It's one of the least attractive aspects of my business that I encounter, but I'm afraid that *all* careers have their pros and cons."

"It sounds as though there are more cons in real estate than donut making, and I mean the kind of con that's been in jail."

"Clever," Momma said with a shrug. "If you don't mind, I believe I'll take this opportunity to go up to my room and make a few phone calls. You'll excuse me, won't you?"

"Of course," I said, and then I added, "Momma, I didn't mean to offend you just now with what I said about your chosen profession."

She looked startled by my comment. "Dear girl, it would take a great deal more than that to offend me, especially coming from you. I'm not blind to the seedier sides of how I make my livelihood, but I still find it the most exhilarating way to spend my days, or I wouldn't keep doing it."

"Okay. As long as we're good," I said.

"Good as gold," Momma said and then she patted my shoulder before she went upstairs.

That kind of left me on my own. I didn't want to go back to the room I was sharing with Jake, and I certainly didn't want to be a fourth wheel at that breakfast meeting, so I decided to wander around and check out the inn a little more closely since our time there was running out. Walking down the hall between the dining room and the lobby, I let my gaze linger over the old photographs that lined the walkway. I'd seen them the day before, but I hadn't really noticed them. They had all clearly been taken in the past, and they showed various aspects of life in Devil's Ridge. On second thought, I really couldn't say whether they were all old or not. The black-and-white development made *everything* look dated, though a few shots were clearly newer than some of the others.

I almost missed it the first time I saw it.

I had walked by one of the photographs, glancing at it without really taking it in, before moving on to the next one.

Three photographs later, I realized what I'd just seen.

Hurrying back, I stood in front of the photo, taking in the scene. It was of a hiking trail in the mountains, clearly on the outside of town. The photo showed a graveled path as well as a small marker made of wood designating the completion of the first mile of the course.

The sign said DR1.

I wasn't sure what the last 01 meant, but I had a hunch I'd just found the location where the Southern Shooting Star had been buried by a criminal desperate to hide his treasure before law enforcement caught up with him.

Why Tommy Gun had been on a hiking trail at all was beyond me. Maybe he was trying to get away on foot, but that didn't make sense. He'd been captured in town, not out in the woods on an old trail. Still, the sign I was looking at was too good a clue not to be true.

Unless I missed my guess, the artifact was buried just below the surface, right under the marker I was looking at.

I took a picture of the black-and-white photograph with my phone, and then I sent it to Momma, Jake, and Phillip at the same time, with the identical caption. "I found DR1. Meet me in the lobby as soon as possible."

I'll say this for my family. Once I made my announcement, it didn't take long for them to congregate.

To my surprise, Momma was first.

"Where did you find that, Suzanne?" she asked.

I pointed to the sign. "It was right under our noses the entire time."

She looked at it and then shook her head in amazement. "I've walked by this photograph a dozen times since we've been here, and I never noticed it, not once."

"Don't feel bad, Momma. I almost missed it myself."

"Perhaps, but the important thing is that you didn't. That is fine work, Suzanne."

I wasn't about to argue the point with her as Phillip and Jake rushed toward us from the dining room.

"Where's the deputy sheriff?" I asked them.

"He had to go," Phillip said. "Where is it?"

As I pointed it out to both men, Jake said with a grin, "After we made excuses and left first." He looked at the photo, and then he smiled at me. "Nice spot, Suzanne."

"It feels a little wonky though, doesn't it?" I asked them.

"What do you mean?" Phillip asked, still eagerly staring at the photograph, as though it held a secret if only he studied it long and hard enough.

"You know more about Tommy Gun than any of us," I told him. "Does it make sense to you that he was hiking on a trail with the police on his tail?"

"I've seen men run toward much stranger places than that when someone is in pursuit," Jake said.

"I have, too," Phillip echoed. "This *has* to be it."

"Well, there's only one way to find out," I said. "Let's go find this trail and do a little digging."

"I'm ready if you are," Momma said. "What do you suppose the 01 means?"

"The Star could have been buried a foot down under the sign," Phillip suggested.

"Or a foot away from it, more likely," Jake answered.

"Why do you say that?"

"I'm guessing Tommy Gun wasn't carrying around a shovel with him, so he probably had to dig with his hands. It's a good thing, too, because I have a feeling the ground is going to be too hard a foot down for us to find it until spring."

"Then we make a circle around the signpost and dig down a foot in all directions," Phillip said as he tapped the photo's glass with his knuckle. "We're close. I can feel it."

"I hope it's not just another wild goose chase," I said.

"Suzanne, why are you so reticent now? After all, you're the one who called this to our attention, and yet you act as though you don't believe it's true."

"I'm not sure," I said. "Maybe I'm just a little gun-shy," I answered. "After all, we've been burned before."

"Well, we can stand around here debating it for an hour or two, or we can do what I want to do and go start digging," Phillip said with a grin. "We'll know soon enough, so why question it? Is everyone else ready?"

"Let's do it," I said.

We were almost out the door when Jimmy Garrett called out to us.

"Should we just keep walking and pretend we didn't hear him?" I asked softly. We had a mission again, and I for one didn't want to wait a second longer to see if I was right or wrong about the Star's resting place.

"We have to stop," Momma said, pivoting around. "Good morning, Mr. Garrett. We'd love to chat, but we're going for another drive."

"You folks sure do love to drive around town," he said, smiling softly. From his perspective, it was probably true, since we'd used the same excuse the night before.

"What can I say? We have limited interests," I said with a smile. "Has Joy shown up today?"

"I'm afraid he hasn't," the innkeeper said.

"Do you think he's gone for good?" Phillip asked.

"If he is, I feel as though it's a pretty safe bet that he's one of the people trying to drive me out of business, but I'm resolved now to hang on until the bitter end, even if it means losing everything."

I had to admire his resolution, and I knew that I'd feel the same way about the donut shop if our roles had been reversed. A captain going down with her ship was for more than sailors, I knew.

"Well, if we can help, be sure to let us know," Phillip said as he started for the door.

"Be careful in the parking lot," Mr. Garrett warned us. "I've got a man coming with rock salt to treat the entire area. There are a few spots of black ice, and the snow is beginning to fall."

"We saw it on our way back from the DINE," I told him.

The innkeeper looked a little put off by the news. "Why didn't you eat with us? Is the food not up to your standards?"

"It's not that," I said, but I didn't want to get into the real reason Momma and I had gone there. Instead, I winked at him conspiratorially and said softly, "I had to go there to deliver a warning."

He looked surprised to hear that. "A warning? To whom?"

"The Liar's Club," I told him.

"What did you say to them?" Garrett asked me, clearly unsure how to take me. That was okay; most of the folks in April Springs didn't know how to deal with me, so why should he be any different?

"I just let them know that we were onto them," I said.

"Did you give them any specifics?" the innkeeper asked.

"No, I left it all kind of vague. I wanted their imaginations to run a little wild. Unless I miss my guess, you won't be having any more trouble with any of them."

"I hope you're right," he said. "I sincerely hope so."

We were out in the parking lot heading to my Jeep when it happened.

I didn't even see the patch of black ice, but Phillip's feet found it, and with a whoop of surprise, I watched as his legs went out from under him, and he hit the pavement of the parking lot, hard.

Chapter 14

"ARE YOU OKAY?" I ASKED my stepfather as I rushed to him, being careful to skirt the slick pavement. I'd come close to wiping out myself in the parking lot of the DINE, and I didn't want to join him flat on my back on the ground now. If Phillip had been moving a bit more slowly, he might have caught himself, but in his rush to get to the Devil's Ridge trail, he'd taken his eyes off the ground, and he'd lost his footing.

"I think so," he said as he tried to sit up.

He couldn't do it, though.

"Suzanne, go get help," Momma said as she tried to comfort her husband.

"I'm okay, Dot," he insisted. "Nothing's broken. I can walk."

He sat up again, and then his hand went to the back of his head. "Okay, maybe I'm not okay. I hit pretty hard."

"We need to get you medical attention," she said.

I had started back toward the inn when Mr. Garrett came rushing out. "I saw it all. I've already called for an ambulance. I'm so sorry."

"Hey, you warned us," Phillip said, trying to smile in spite of his pain. "I was just in too big a hurry to pay attention."

In the distance, I could hear a siren. Phillip motioned to Jake and me, and we bent down on either side of him so we could hear his softened voice.

"What is it?" Jake asked him.

"Go get the Star," he said quietly.

"What? You're out of your mind. We're going to the hospital with you," I said.

Jake agreed. "It's waited this long, Phillip. It can wait a little longer."

"Look up into the sky," Phillip said. "It's really starting to snow. If the Star gets buried in snow and ice, when will we be able to go back to get it? The trail will probably be closed for the winter soon, and I won't be able to rest until we know one way or the other if we were right."

I wanted to stay with him, and clearly so did Jake, so it surprised me when Momma said, "Do as he asks, children."

It was an odd thing to call us, Jake more so than me. "Seriously?" I asked her.

"Seriously," she said firmly. "There's nothing you can do for him at the hospital, and this is what he wants."

"Jake?" I asked. "What do you think?"

"If the roles were reversed, I'd be urging you all to do the same thing," he admitted.

"So would I," I said before turning back to Phillip. "Are you sure?"

"I'm positive," he said. Trying to grin yet again, he added, "Happy hunting, and bring me back a Star."

The innkeeper was hovering nearby, and he must have thought Phillip was delusional asking for a star while he was lying on his back in a hotel parking lot.

"The ambulance is here," he said. "You'll be okay soon enough."

"Go," Phillip urged us yet again.

I wasn't sure if the glaze in his eyes was from a possible concussion or from the prospect that we were hopefully about to recover the object of his dreams for him.

Either way, I knew that Jake and I had no choice, and from the rate the snow was coming down, it was clearly going to have to be sooner rather than later.

"We'll see you soon," I said as I squeezed his hand, and then, totally on impulse, I leaned forward and kissed his cheek. "Feel better."

"I already do," he said with a slight smile. I looked up to see Momma smiling at me too.

This was getting entirely too sentimental for my taste.

"Let's go," I told Jake as I stood.

"Race you to the Jeep," he said with a laugh.

"Why don't we hold off on any footraces until we're on more solid ground?" I suggested.

"That's probably a good idea."

As we got into the Jeep and I started the engine, I turned on the windshield wipers and dismissed the fallen snow from it.

"I'm suddenly glad we brought your Jeep after all," Jake said with a grin.

"There you go. I knew you'd come around," I said as I pulled out of the parking lot. In my rearview mirror, I saw some EMTs seeing to my stepfather, but I couldn't think about that at the moment.

I had to focus every ounce of energy I had on not getting us killed, at least until we knew for sure whether we were about to find treasure or fool's gold instead.

"By the way, how was breakfast?" I asked Jake as I started to get a better handle on driving in the falling snow. It wasn't just snow, which was the real problem. There was freezing rain mixed in, a little sleet, and, at times, some icy cold rain as well. All in all, it made for a messy drive, and I wasn't looking forward to getting out of the Jeep and hiking a mile in this weather, but hopefully we'd be rewarded for our efforts in the end.

"It was good," Jake said. "We all traded war stories. Usual cop stuff. How was yours?" he asked me.

"Breakfast was good. We *have* to go there someday. Their pancakes are unbelievable."

"Sounds good," Jake said absently. His mind was clearly on other things. "Do you still have that folding shovel in back?"

"I don't go anywhere without it," I said. "You never know when you're going to need it with the way our weather can change."

"I was thinking we'd take it with us to the mile marker and use it to dig. Just because Tommy Gun didn't have one doesn't mean that we can't use it."

"Sounds good to me," I said.

"So, breakfast was good? Did anything interesting happen while you were there?"

"A couple of things, actually," I said. "On our way out, Momma and I stopped at the Liar's Club table, and I let them know that we were onto them."

"Did you identify who exactly the 'we' you were talking about was?" he asked me, keeping his gaze on the road as carefully as I was.

"I left it open so their imaginations could go to work," I admitted.

He grinned. "Nice. What else happened?"

"Technically it happened before we even got into the diner," I told him. "I had to park between two monster trucks that were jacked up halfway to the sky. As Momma and I started around the corner, we heard two people arguing. It sounded pretty intense."

"Really? What were they arguing about?" Jake asked as he watched out the window, clearly just making conversation.

"This skinny guy named Henry said that he wanted to go home, but this big brute he was with named Mr. Duncan told him they weren't going anywhere until they got what they came for. Oh, I forgot to tell you, they were driving a black SUV, too."

That got his attention. "Like the one we saw before in the Overlook parking lot?"

"It looked a lot like it, but I couldn't say for sure. It was going too fast out of there for us to catch the license plate. Honestly, I thought the little guy with the blue hair was going to cut and run for a second there."

"What? He had blue hair?" Jake asked, now intently interested.

"Yes, didn't I mention that before?"

"You did not. And you said that his name was Henry?" Jake followed up.

"That's what that guy named Duncan called him," I admitted. "Why, is that significant?"

"A guy named Henry with blue hair is the one who sold Phillip the letters and papers that belonged to Tommy Malone," Jake said. "Apparently now he's decided to do a little treasure hunting himself."

"Who are you calling?" I asked as I pulled into the parking lot for the Devil's Ridge Loop Hiking Trail, its official name. At least that was what the big sign said. No other vehicle was parked in the lot, which wasn't that big a surprise, given the weather. Nobody in their right mind would be out today if they could help it.

"I want to talk to Phillip," he said. After a few moments, he said, "There's no answer."

"Try Momma," I suggested.

He did as I suggested, but after another moment, he put his phone away. "It went straight to voicemail."

"We'll tell them later," I said as I opened my door and felt the cold rush in. "Are you ready for this?"

"I'm as ready as I'll ever be," he said.

"Then let's grab my shovel and go."

The trail was worse than I thought, and as we made our way up the hill, I started to wonder if this was such a good idea after all. At least the sleet and freezing rain were letting up. That was the good news. The bad? The snow was coming down hard now, covering everything with a speed I'd never seen before. "Do we turn back, or should we keep going?" I asked Jake.

"We shouldn't have far to go now," he said as he slipped a bit, hitting a patch of ice just under the fresh layer of snow.

"I hope not," I said. As we continued on, the snow got deeper and deeper, and I could feel it easing up to the tops of my tennis shoes and into my socks. I'd thought about wearing hiking boots for the trip, but I'd changed my mind at the last minute. After all, how could I have possibly known that I'd be hiking in the snow? The worst part was that I'd pulled a pair of rubber boots out of the back that I used when it was muddy out. I'd mistakenly thought I was done with them for the season.

My foot slipped, and Jake caught me just in time. We'd been gaining in elevation since we'd left the parking lot, and the sides of the trail were getting steeper and steeper. One wrong step, and I'd be plummeting down the side of the mountain, which didn't seem like my idea of a good time at all.

Finally, after what seemed like hours, we crested the hill we were on and saw the sign.

DR1.

It was just as it had appeared in the photograph, only now the top of it was crusted with snow.

Jake and I made a one-foot circle around the sign, and then we took turns digging up the soil underneath it. Fortunately there was a layer of leaves just below the snow, and it had served to insulate the ground a little, so at least we could still turn it over.

"How far down should we go?" I asked him as I took my turn on the shovel, upon my insistence and his resistance.

"Not more than two or three inches," he said. "Even if the ground was soft when Tommy buried the Star, I doubt he'd be able to go much deeper than that, even if he used a tree branch or something to help him dig."

"Got it," I said. I worked some of the circle, and then Jake insisted on taking over.

I probably should have fought his suggestion a little harder, but I was sweating under my heavy coat, and my arms were already getting a bit rubbery.

As he worked with the efficient movements I'd grown used to, I asked him, "I wonder what the park rangers are going to think when they see our handiwork?"

"I'm guessing it will be a few weeks or even months before that happens, and we'll be long gone by then," he said.

His shovel bit hard into something that clearly wasn't soil when we were nearly all of the way around the circle, and he stopped digging abruptly.

"I just hit something," Jake said excitedly.

His digging became more delicate as he struggled to unearth what we hoped was hidden treasure, and I found myself holding my breath, waiting to see what he was about to uncover.

Chapter 15

"WHAT IS IT? DID YOU find the Star?" I asked as I heard footsteps suddenly coming up from behind us. We were vulnerable at the moment, both of us kneeling down, trying to uncover what had been buried just beneath the ground.

"That's far enough," a voice I'd heard before said. "Why don't you two stand up and move away from the Star?"

It was Duncan, and standing a step behind him was the blue-haired man, Henry. He was unarmed and shivering in the cold weather, but the big man beside him didn't look one bit inconvenienced by the snow.

The gun in his hand looked massive, at least it did as I stared down the barrel of it. Jake hadn't even had time to get his own weapon out.

We were caught flat-footed, and from the look of things, it was a pretty safe bet that we were about to die.

Chapter 16

"I UNDERSTAND WHY YOU were in town," I said, trying to keep from staring at the handgun pointing at us, "but how did you know about the clue we found in the brick wall?"

"What wall? Oh, you're talking about back at the old library. We didn't know," he said.

"Then how is it that you're here?" Jake asked him.

"It's simple enough. We followed you," Duncan said. "In fact, we've been following you for a while. Don't beat yourself up if you didn't see us. I'm pretty good at tailing people without them knowing it. It goes to my particular skill set, if you know what I mean."

Was he actually bragging to us? I wanted to wipe that smug look off his face, but unfortunately, that wasn't going to happen.

"What about you, Henry? If there's one thing I hate, it's a dishonorable crook," Jake told the slim man with so much scorn in his voice that it snapped the young man's head back.

"He made me do it!" Henry protested. "I was bragging at the bar about the suckers I sold my family's letters to, and how I'd pawned off everything *twice* but still kept copies for myself. I wasn't used to having money in my pocket, and I might have gotten a little drunk."

"I heard him shooting off his mouth, and I realized that we could get to the Star first if we played our cards right," Duncan finished. "Tell you what. Why don't you get back down on your hands and knees and keep digging for us?"

"Why should I?" Jake asked, his voice calm and cool. "You're just going to shoot us when we dig it up, so I don't see why we should help you get it."

"Maybe, maybe not," Duncan said completely failing to convince anyone there that he wasn't planning to kill us as soon as he had the Star in his hands. "But wouldn't you at least like to delay the inevitable, even if it's true?"

"Hang on! You never said anything about killing anyone!" Henry protested.

"If you don't shut your mouth, I'll take care of you as soon as I'm finished with them."

"You wouldn't dare," Henry said, but it was clear to all of us that it had been his plan all along. After all, what did Duncan need Henry for once he had the Southern Shooting Star in his possession? The heir to Tommy Gun would just be one more liability at that point.

"Don't push me, then."

Jake must have been coming up with a plan since we'd first realized that we'd been trapped there, but when he acted, I hadn't been expecting it in the least.

Before I realized what was happening, I felt him tackling me and pushing me over the edge of the trail to what felt like the abyss below.

As we slid down the slope among the trees, I could hear shouting from above us, and two shots rang out above our heads.

"Keep going downhill," Jake told me, panting, as I started to slow on the slope where the snow hadn't quite had a chance to build up yet. "There's got to be something down there."

"Okay," I said. "Thanks for pushing me off the side of a cliff," I said.

"I didn't push you, I tackled you," he said as we continued to scramble downward.

There was another shot, and then Jake stopped himself against a tree, pulled out his own handgun, and fired into a nearby embankment.

The sound was deafening so close, and as the dirt and snow puffed up, I felt my ears ringing.

"Sorry, I should have warned you first," Jake said.

"Why didn't you shoot back at him?" I asked.

"I couldn't risk it," he said.

"Then what was the point of shooting at all?" I asked.

"I wanted him to know that I was armed, too," Jake said. "Let's keep moving."

We had been going another ten minutes when I heard a scream of frustration coming from above us. "It's just a rock, you idiots. The Star isn't here!"

I looked at Jake, and despite being cold, wet, and exhausted from our descent, I grinned at him. "We may not have found the Star, but neither did he."

"No, but he's going to come after us now, whether I'm armed or not," Jake replied, increasing his pace.

As we moved, I could swear I heard footfalls coming down the side of the hill toward us in the fresh snow. "They're coming after us, aren't they?" I asked as Jake pointed to a widened spot in the trees. It was another trail!

"We'll make better time now," he said.

"But which direction do we go in?" I asked him. "I'm all turned around."

"I'm guessing the sun's over that way, even given how overcast it is, so that means this trail runs north/south. If we follow this, we'll get back to the parking lot or the road soon enough."

"How confident are you in that prediction?" I asked him as we set off in the direction he'd just indicated.

All Jake could do was shrug. "There are no guarantees in this life, Suzanne. You know that. Right now, it's just the best we can do."

"Then let's go fast," I said as I tried to double my pace, which was slower than normal but faster than I'd been picking my way down a mountain. "At least we're on flat ground," I said.

"Don't look to your left, then," Jake said.

I did anyway, and saw that there was an even steeper drop-off there now. I knew that we'd been climbing in elevation in the Jeep since we'd left town, but I'd had no idea just how much. Every time I brushed against a tree along the edge, snow hit me, dowsing me once again. I was still running on adrenaline—being chased by a bad guy had a tendency to do that to me—but I knew that I'd be running out of steam soon enough.

The woods around us were suddenly silent.

"Did we lose them?"

"No, they're still behind us," he said. "Keep moving."

"I'm right beside you," I said, though it was clear to me that I was starting to fade, and fast.

"Keep moving, Suzanne," he reminded me as he reached over and took my hand. "We'll get out of this yet."

"I hope so," I said, and just the contact from us holding hands was enough to bolster my spirits. Even if we didn't make it out of this alive, at least I'd be with my husband in the end, and I found a surprising amount of solace in that fact.

But I wasn't quite ready to just give up yet.

Chapter 17

I WAS LOST IN MY OWN thoughts, stumbling along in the snow and listening intently behind us when Jake's shout brought me out of my funk.

"Suzanne, we made it!" Jake said happily. "Look! There's your Jeep."

I'd never been so happy to see it in my life. As we walked up the lower loop of the trail back to the parking lot, I could already feel my feet warming up. The next time I left the house, even if it was ninety degrees out, I was going to be prepared for cold weather, just in case. This trek had convinced me of that.

Jake pointed to the tire tracks in the snow beside our Jeep. "They've been here and gone already," Jake said. "They must not have been following us in the snow after all."

"I could swear I heard someone behind us," I told him.

"I thought so, too, but by the amount of snow in their tracks, it's pretty clear that they're long gone."

"But not forgotten," I said as I noticed something that made my heart sink.

Evidently Duncan had left us a calling card before he'd taken off, with or without his unwilling accomplice.

All four tires of my Jeep had been slashed.

We weren't going anywhere.

Chapter 18

I PULLED MY CELL PHONE out as Jake inspected the tires. I didn't need to look at them. There was no doubt in my mind that they were beyond salvaging.

To make matters worse, if that were possible, there was no signal on my phone.

"Try your phone," I told Jake. "I can't get out."

He did, and then frowned at me. "I don't have a signal, either."

"Well, we can't drive out of here, not on my rims, but I'm not ready for another hike just yet," I told him. "Why don't we sit in the Jeep, turn the heat on, and get warmed up a little before we head out for help?"

"That sounds like a good plan to me," Jake said.

My attitude started to improve the moment my feet began to thaw. "Can we just stay here and forget about everything else?"

"Do you mean for another hour or two, or until spring?" Jake asked with a slight smile.

"Well, at least until it stops snowing," I answered.

"I'd love to, but I don't like the idea of Duncan being out there on the loose," Jake said. "Henry's clearly told him about Phillip, so I have to make sure that he and your mother are safe."

I hadn't even thought about that. "You're right. Let's get ready and go," I said as I put my still-wet shoes and socks back on. I'd taken them off earlier so I could rub them warm again, but it was agony putting them back on in their condition. I wasn't worried so much about my own comfort at the moment, though.

I was worried about Phillip and Momma.

We finished getting dressed, got out of the Jeep, and started down the short drive to the main road we'd taken a few hours earlier, though it felt at that moment as though it had been days.

In the end, we didn't have far to walk after all.

A Devil's Ridge squad car pulled up behind us less than ten minutes after we'd left my Jeep. Jake's breakfast buddy rolled down his window and grinned up at us. "Do you two need a lift?"

"We'd appreciate it," Jake said as we both climbed into the front of the cruiser. It was a tight fit, but I wasn't in any mood to sit in back, and I knew that I couldn't ask Jake to.

"What happened? Break down in the snow?" he asked good-naturedly.

"As a matter of fact, someone slashed all four of our tires right after they tried to kill us," Jake told him.

"They tried to kill you? Those blasted kids are getting worse and worse every day. I don't know why they think it's okay to destroy other people's property, but they do."

"It wasn't kids," Jake said. "Let me tell you what's been going on."

After Jake caught him up on what we'd been up to, including looking for the Southern Shooting Star, the deputy whistled softly. "Hang on. I need to process this for a second," he said. After nearly a full minute, he got out his radio and started barking orders. First he had his dispatcher call the Overlook, where he got the black SUV's license plate, and then he had the dispatcher contact everyone within earshot to be on the lookout for that vehicle and those two men as well. They were armed and dangerous, he warned them, and I for one could vouch for that, at least about Duncan. The deputy sheriff added a bit somberly that it might be just one large heavyset man traveling alone, and as a final thought, he sent one of his people back up the trail to look for Henry's body to see if it was lying somewhere in the snow. It was a grim reminder that Duncan had been playing for keeps, and if it hadn't been for Jake's quick thinking, it might have been three bodies being slowly covered with snow, not one.

"That was well done," Jake told Deputy Alexander after he finished.

"Thanks," he said absently. "Folks around here have been looking for that Star for ages," he said. "Personally, I think it's all a load of hooey."

"How did they even know the Star was in town?" I asked him.

"It's been common knowledge for a whole lot of years that old Tommy Gun Malone had it with him just before he got caught. He showed it off to Juanita Henderson at the DINE, no doubt trying to impress her, not an hour before they nabbed him."

Phillip would be alarmed to hear that he hadn't been the first to know about the Star being in Devil's Ridge after all, but since it was still missing, it didn't seem to matter nearly as much that the entire town had known about it first.

"I'll send a truck out for your Jeep. They'll make quick work of it," Alexander said, and after he had that taken care of, he asked, "Where should I drop you, back at the Overlook?"

"Actually, we need to go to the hospital," Jake said softly.

The deputy was so startled that he nearly drove off the road, but when he got the cruiser back under control, he asked, "What happened? Did he clip one of you? I don't see any blood."

"It's not for us," Jake said. "I just want to make sure Duncan doesn't go after my father-in-law."

Alexander eased up considerably. "There's no way that man's going back to Devil's Ridge, not after what you just told me. There's no doubt in my mind that he's long gone by now."

"Maybe, maybe not," Jake said. "But we still need to get there fast."

Alexander nodded. "I understand, but how about this? I'll call ahead and put a guard on his room, and in the meantime, we go back to the Overlook so you can both take hot showers and get out of those wet clothes. Once you've done that, I'll be more than happy to drive you to the hospital myself. You don't want to mess around and get pneumonia when it's so easily preventable."

"What do you think, Suzanne?" Jake asked me.

A hot shower and fresh clothes sounded like a little bit of heaven to me, but I didn't want to do it if it might put my family in jeopardy. "I'm okay if you want to go straight to the hospital."

Jake seemed to ponder it, and then he asked Alexander, "How good is the man you're sending to guard him?"

"As a matter of fact, he's a she, and she's the best officer on the force, bar none. I can say that because she's my sister, and I tell you truthfully, there's nobody I'd rather have watching my back than Amelia."

"Okay then, we'll do it your way," Jake conceded.

Once we were back at the Overlook Inn, Mr. Garrett was there waiting anxiously for us. "I understand you had car trouble," he said as he studied us for a few moments. Jake and I had gotten dirty from the long slide down the hill, and our clothes were both soaked.

"In a way, I guess that's true," I said.

"I'm going to hang around so they can take a quick shower and change clothes, and then we're going to go see her daddy in the hospital," the deputy said.

"Actually, he's my stepfather," I corrected him automatically. It wasn't that I wasn't fond of Phillip, but I'd had a wonderful father, at least wonderful to me, and I didn't want him to ever be forgotten.

"My mistake," the deputy said, tipping his hat toward me. "Anyway, I'll be here when you're ready, folks."

"That won't be necessary," Mr. Garrett said. "They can borrow my vehicle until theirs is repaired."

"We don't want to put you out," Jake said.

"It's no trouble at all. Even though my Land Cruiser is built for this kind of weather, I have a terrible fear of driving in the snow, so I can assure you that I won't be going anywhere."

"What do you say?" Jake asked me.

"If you're sure, Mr. Garrett, that would be great," I told him.

"Then it's settled," the innkeeper beamed. "Deputy, there's no reason for you to hang around and miss work. I'm sure you're needed with this snow we're getting."

"Well, I appreciate that," the police officer said. "There's a crook or two out there that I wouldn't mind catching myself. When the sheriff gets back from his vacation, it might be nice showing him that I handled things here just fine without him." The deputy said his good-byes, and then he left us at the Overlook.

"You two must be freezing," Mr. Garrett said as he studied us. "I do hope you brought extra shoes with you."

I was glad that I had. They were my nicest pair of tennis shoes, still entirely inappropriate for the weather, but I wasn't planning on doing any more hiking in the snow on this trip. Jake had a pair of shoes with him as well, just because he was Jake. The man was always prepared for just about anything. "We're covered," he said. "Give us ten minutes, and we'll be ready to head out."

"You can certainly take more time than that if you need to," he said. "Come find me when you're ready, and I'll give you my car keys."

I let Jake take the first shower, and as I did, I stripped down to my underwear and tried to get warm. I wasn't sure that was going to happen again any time soon, but I looked forward to the chance to at least try. Getting out of those wet clothes was a huge step in the right direction, and after my shower, I felt amazing. I was glad that we had a virtually unlimited supply of hot water. I'd completely blown our goal of getting out of there quickly, but by the time I was ready to leave the Overlook, I was finally starting to thaw out again.

"Here are the keys," the innkeeper said as he handed them to Jake, not me. I thought it was a bit odd, and I must have smiled, which Mr. Garrett managed to catch. "I didn't mean anything by it," he said. "I just figured that given the fact that your husband was on the State Police, he'd rather drive."

"Suzanne drove us up here," Jake said. "She's an excellent driver."

"Of course she is," he said, clearly debating about whether to try to take the keys from my husband and give them to me instead.

"It's fine," I said. "Thanks for the use of your vehicle, Mr. Garrett."

"Please, I don't know why I didn't ask you before, but call me Jimmy."

"Okay then, thanks, Jimmy," I said with a grin.

"Of course. Please tell your stepfather that I hope he has a quick recovery. I'm afraid this is the last straw. If he sues the inn, I'm not going to have any choice but to shut the place down and hand the keys back over to the bank."

"I can't speak for Phillip," Jake said, "but I'd be shocked if the thought of suing you even crossed his mind. You warned him about the ice, but he fell anyway. I can't imagine him holding you accountable."

"Neither can I," I said. I patted the innkeeper's shoulder. "Don't worry about it, Jimmy. Everything's going to work out in the end."

"If only you saying it would make it true," he said.

"Hey, I always say, where there's life, there's hope," I encouraged him. "Come on, Jake. Let's go."

"Sure," my husband said, but before we left, he asked Jimmy, "I'm curious about something. Have you heard the rumor that Tommy Gun Malone stashed something here in town just before he was captured by police back in the sixties?"

The innkeeper nodded. "You're talking about the Southern Shooting Star. Sure, everybody knows about that, though I'm surprised you do. I thought that was our own little secret around here. There's a rumor that he even stayed here at the inn for a night or two, but I've never been able to confirm it."

"Have you ever looked for the Star yourself?" Jake asked him.

"Me? I'm an innkeeper, not a treasure hunter. I thought I struck gold when I bought *this* place, but it turns out that I was wrong. Anyway, tell Phillip I hope he feels better soon. Oh, and as long as you're in Devil's Ridge, you've got a place to stay, on the house."

"I'm sure my mother will have something to say about that," I told him. "She doesn't believe there's such a thing as a free lunch."

"I wasn't offering you food, just your room," Jimmy said, clearly unfamiliar with the phrase.

"You can take it up with her the next time you see her," I said with a smile.

"Why did you ask him about the Star?" I asked Jake as he drove us to the hospital.

"I wanted to be sure that Deputy Alexander was telling the truth about folks around here already knowing about the Star," Jake said.

"Don't you trust *anybody*?" I asked him with a grin.

"You all of the time, your mother most of the time, and Phillip, too. Fourth would probably be George Morris, and after that, it's a pretty slim list."

"I'll have to tell the mayor that he made the cut," I told Jake. "He'll be honored."

"On second thought, you'd better not say anything to him," Jake answered with a grin. "I'd hate for him to get a big head over it."

"So, we can assume it's true that everyone around here knows about the Star," I said. "Does that change what we think, or what we should do next?"

"As a matter of fact, it makes things even that much more hopeless," Jake admitted.

"How so?"

"If folks around here have been looking for the Star for that long, what hope do we have? I thought Phillip had something with that coded letter of his, and then I found that note buried in the wall in front of the library instead of the treasure we were looking for. I lost hope, and then you spotted that photograph at the inn that seemed to fit, but it's clearly not there, either. I'm afraid old Tommy Gun was a little too clever for his own good. Unless I miss my guess, the Star is either going to be found completely by accident, or nobody's ever going to recover it."

"You're probably right," I said as I cranked up the heater another notch. It was probably too hot in the Land Cruiser as it was, but I didn't care. I had a chill in my bones that I was trying to get rid of. "What would we do with that kind of money, anyway? It would probably just bring us more problems than we need."

"Funny you should say that. We were going to turn it over to the insurance company and split the reward four ways," Jake said as he concentrated on the road. It was definitely getting slicker now, and I was happy we were in such a reliable vehicle when it came to traveling in the snow.

"But what if nobody already owned it?" I asked. "What would we do with it then, if the Star was all ours?"

"We'd probably stick it in a museum so everyone could enjoy it," Jake said.

"That's a really nice idea," I said as I snuggled a bit closer to my husband. My seat belt kept me from getting too close, but I liked being near the man. "I would have liked to see that."

"Then it's settled," Jake said. "Now all we have to do is to find the blasted thing, which we both know is not going to happen, and then convince the real owners to put it back on display, even though it was stolen the last time that happened. Easy as pie," he added with a grin.

"You must be Amelia," Jake said to the wary cop who stood up from her chair in front of the door to my stepfather's room the moment we appeared. "I'm Jake Bishop, and this is my wife, Suzanne."

"Have any ID on you?" she asked, not budging an inch.

"I've got it right here," Jake said with a slight grin.

"Hold on," she said, taking him in quickly. "You're armed."

"I used to be with the North Carolina State Police. I'm usually armed. If you're okay with it, I'm going to get my wallet out now, but I won't make any sudden moves."

I thought he was joking, at least until I saw Officer Amelia's intent expression. I suddenly realized that she hadn't taken her hand off the butt of her revolver. Wow, she really *was* intense.

After she was satisfied with Jake's identification, she handed it back and pointed to me. "Now you."

I was about to protest when I glanced at Jake. He nodded slightly, so instead of commenting, I did as I'd been asked and showed her my driver's license.

Only then did she ease her hand off of her weapon. "You can't ever be too careful," she said. If it was an apology, it wasn't much of one, but Jake seemed to think it was just right.

"I appreciate you being so thorough," he said. "Are you taking off now?"

"No, not until I hear from the acting sheriff," she said as she settled back into the chair where she'd been sitting when we'd arrived.

"Then we'll see you soon," Jake said as we went into Phillip's room to visit the patient. I wasn't sure what I was expecting, but when we got inside, it was still quite a shock to see my stepfather in a hospital gown again.

Chapter 19

"HOW ARE YOU DOING?" I asked Phillip as I leaned over and kissed his cheek again. It was getting to be a habit with me, but I was truly glad to see him.

"Did you meet my watchdog outside?" he asked me with a grin. "She practically frisked my doctor before she'd let him in." He looked good; his color was strong, and his eyes were clear.

"Good for her," I said as I hugged Momma. "How is he doing, really?"

"He is fine," Phillip answered for her, "and he's ready to get his trousers back and get out of here."

"They're keeping him tonight for observation," Momma said.

"Which is insane," Phillip retorted. "I'm perfect, fit as a fiddle."

"You took a pretty sound blow to the head, and unless you want another one, you'll start cooperating," Momma said with a teasing demeanor.

"Yes, ma'am," he said with the hint of a grin.

"What was that?" she asked, feigning sternness.

"Yes, dear? Yes, Dot? Why don't you feed me the right lines so I don't blow them the next time?"

"He seems okay to me," I said.

"There! I told you!"

"Don't encourage him," Momma said. "We heard what happened on the trail. I'm so sorry we weren't there with you. The deputy sheriff stopped by ten minutes ago to bring us up to speed on what's been going on. It's a miracle you two are safe after all of that."

"If Jake hadn't tackled me and thrown me off a cliff, I probably wouldn't be here right now," I said with a grin.

"She's exaggerating," Jake supplied swiftly. "We both went over the embankment together. It wasn't really what you could call a cliff."

"But that bully named Duncan still shot at you, twice, correct?" Momma asked him.

"Yes, that part was true enough," Jake answered.

She took his shoulders in her hands and kissed him soundly on the lips, something that startled both Jake and me, but evidently not Phillip. He just grinned, but he didn't say a word. Momma said formally, "Thank you for saving my daughter again."

"You're welcome, but to be fair, she's saved me right back just as many times," Jake answered.

Phillip stared off into space for a few seconds before speaking. "So, we've hit our last dead end."

"I'm afraid so," Jake said as he put his hand on Phillip's shoulder. "There was nothing there. There's something else you should know, too."

"What, that the entire town already knows that the Southern Shooting Star was stashed somewhere around here long before I found out?" Phillip asked him with a wry grin. "Alexander told me. Oh, well. At least we tried, and as a bonus, nobody got killed this time."

"At least not so far," Momma said under her breath. I didn't think anyone else heard her, but I surely did.

"What happens next?" I asked, trying to ease the tension in the room a bit.

"Tomorrow, as soon as I get out of here, we check out of the inn, get in our vehicles, and go home with our tails between our legs," Phillip said. "That is, if you all are okay with giving up now."

The chorus of yeses was loud, strong, and immediate.

Phillip smiled again. "If I'm going to be a loser, there isn't anybody else in the world I'd want to be a loser with than the three of you."

"Then it's settled," I said. "Momma, are you coming back to the Overlook with us tonight?"

"No, I've made arrangements to sleep here," she said as she pointed to the empty bed beside Phillip's. "They've been most kind about it."

"Did they really have much choice, Dot?" Phillip asked.

"They most certainly did," Momma said a bit stiffly.

"My darling wife, I love you with all of my heart, but when you get that edge in your voice and that look in your eye, you terrify even me. How about you, Suzanne? You know what I'm talking about, so don't try to deny it."

I kissed her cheek before I said, "Momma, sometimes you could scare the brass off a bell."

She took that in, and then turned to my husband. "Jacob? Do you feel that way as well?"

It was clear he didn't want to answer, but finally, he had to, after being under her steady stare for nearly a minute. I couldn't believe that he'd lasted that long. I know that I never had. "Dot, even when I'm armed to the teeth, I'm careful around you when you want your way."

"So, you all think I'm some kind of a bully?" Momma asked.

"Are you kidding? We *love* you for being so overprotective of us," I said.

I hugged her, and Jake joined in. Phillip started to get up, but Momma shot him a look that settled him back down onto the bed instantly. "Very well," she said. "I won't deny it, then. I'd do anything to protect the three of you."

"Right back at you, Momma," I said. "Listen, I hate to break up the party, but the snow's really coming down out there, and unless Jake and I are planning on bunking in here with the two of you, we'd better head back to the Overlook."

"Be careful, Jake," Momma said as she walked us to the door.

"Always," he replied, and then he spontaneously leaned down and kissed her cheek.

She smiled from the attention, and when we left, Momma and Phillip were arguing about who loved the other one more.

I was happy to see Officer Amelia still on duty.

Jake said, "Don't get up. We're heading back to the Overlook. Thanks for looking out for them."

"Happy to," she said, barely cracking a smile of acknowledgment.

I'd been righter than I'd realized about the snow. When we got back out into the parking lot, Jake had to wipe the windshield clean time and time again before he could see well enough to drive.

It looked as though we were in for one heck of a snowstorm, but at least we'd be warm, and inside, no matter how badly the storm raged outside.

I wouldn't be sad to see Devil's Ridge in my rearview mirror the next day, though, and I hoped that we'd be able to make it back down the mountain and toward home. We'd had a little fun, a fair dose of excitement, and some moments of absolute sheer terror.

All in all, it was a vacation I could have done without taking, and I couldn't wait to get back to Donut Hearts and do something safe again, like make donuts for a living.

"Wow, this snow is really getting crazy," I said as I looked out the window of the Land Cruiser.

"I'm glad we're driving this tank," Jake answered.

"Hey, my Jeep could handle it."

"Don't get defensive," Jake said with a grin. "I hope they got it to the tire place in time. I'd hate to have to wait around for them to dig it out of a snowbank."

"Me, too," I said. I wasn't sure how I was going to pay for four new tires. I might have to turn the claim in to my insurance, but I didn't want to risk making my premiums go up. It was a modern dilemma, there was no doubt about it.

We finally got back to the Overlook Inn, and I started breathing easier the moment Jake shut the engine off. The parking lot had been scraped, but the roads hadn't been plowed yet. Surely a place in the Blue Ridge Mountains would have a way of removing snow.

We made our way inside, and Jimmy Garrett was at the desk, looking anxious about something. "You made it. How is Mr. Martin doing?" he asked us.

"He's ready to break out of the hospital," I said with a smile. "They're keeping him overnight, but he should be discharged tomorrow."

"His truck was dropped off an hour ago, so he'll be all set," the innkeeper said. "I also got a call from the garage about your Jeep. They'll bring it by after work this evening." He looked outside. "I'm hoping you'll at least stay tonight, though. I'd hate for *anyone* to be out on those roads when it turns dark."

"I was a bit surprised that the main road hadn't been plowed yet," Jake said as he took his jacket off and shook the snow off of it.

"The plow got stuck in a snowbank," the innkeeper said with a grin. "There's a new kid operating it, and he somehow managed to get it hung up leaving the storage yard where they keep it. They've got another plow coming from a town a bit farther south, but it won't be here for a few hours."

"We're not planning on going anywhere tonight, anyway," I told him. "I'm hoping you'll be serving dinner in the restaurant this evening."

"Oh, yes. Our cook stays on site in bad weather, so there are no worries there," he said.

"Then we'll be there," Jake said.

As we were leaving the lobby, I saw Nicole and Wesley Langford approach the desk. "We need to check out, and I don't want to hear any nonsense about a late fee tacked onto our bill, either. You don't have anyone coming in during a snowstorm, so don't try to convince me otherwise that you need the rooms we were in."

"No one's coming in," Mr. Garrett said, "but I'm afraid no one's going out, either."

Wesley looked outside. "Why not? It's just a little snow."

"You're welcome to take your chances if you'd like," the innkeeper said with a smile, "but if you decide to stay with us one more night, I'd be happy to see if we could accommodate you. In any case, the roads won't be plowed until midnight."

"Wesley, stop being so stubborn," Nicole said, and then turned to Mr. Garrett. "We'll be staying another night," she told him. "Thank you."

"You are most welcome," he said graciously.

As they walked past us, I could swear that they hadn't even seen us. "Giving up on your hunt?" I asked him the moment he passed by us.

Wesley stopped in his tracks and looked at me. "What are you talking about?"

"You're here looking for the Star, like everyone else," I said.

"Why would I look for something that's clearly not here?" he asked.

"I know that, and my husband knows that, but how do *you* know that?" I asked in all seriousness. Was it possible that the Langfords had been in cahoots with Duncan? It was hard to believe, but I'd seen odder things in my life.

"Wouldn't you like to know?" he asked as he stormed off.

Nicole lingered. "Don't pay any attention to my brother. He just hates being thwarted. He's figured out that the Star is so well hidden at this point no one is going to find it." She seemed to grin a bit as she said it.

"You seem okay with not recovering it," I told her.

"This was never my dream. I just indulged my brother." She started to follow him, and then she stopped and turned to us. "By the way, there's really no mystery involved. He has a police scanner app on his phone, so he's been monitoring everything that's been going on without leaving the comfort of his room. There's been enough chatter that he's picked up what's been happening. For what it's worth, I'm glad you two are all right."

"Thanks. We appreciate that," I said.

Jake was about to add something when Wesley must have finally noticed that his sister wasn't in tow. "Nicole, are you coming?" he asked angrily.

"I'll be right there," she said as she winked at us and hurried to join him.

"So, everyone knows what happened to us today," I said as Jake and I made our way up to our room.

"Hey, it's a small town, Suzanne. I shouldn't have to tell you what that's like. Word travels fast, and you've got to admit, being stranded with four slashed tires after being shot at isn't exactly low profile. What do you think they were talking about before we showed up?"

"Probably nothing as exciting as what happened today," I admitted. I'd been on the other end of that kind of gossip too many times back in April Springs, so I knew that Jake was right. Unless I missed my guess, everyone in Devil's Ridge would know by now that we'd failed yet again to recover the Southern Shooting Star. That was just as well. I would have hated for anyone to come after us thinking that we'd actually found the cursed thing. The hunt had sounded like fun the day before, but I was most earnestly wishing at that moment that Phillip had never brought it up.

Maybe I was just hungry. "Are you ready to eat?" I asked Jake.

"I'm surprised you waited this long to ask me," he replied with a grin.

"That doesn't answer my question though, does it?"

"Let's go," he answered.

The food was tasty enough, but it was mostly lost on me. I couldn't help wondering how long this snow would last, and if we'd even be able to get out of there in the morning. The last thing I wanted to do was miss my next shift at the donut shop. It was my oasis in a sea of insanity, and it felt as though nothing bad could happen to me if I was in the kitchen making tasty treats. I knew that wasn't true, since I'd been attacked in my shop on more than one occasion, but it was how I felt anyway.

After dinner, Jake and I spent some time in the lobby enjoying the blazing fire and watching the snow come down outside the windows. Jimmy had the outside floodlights turned on near the edge of the drop-off to the right where the fireplace windows were, and it was fascinating watching the cascade of flakes dance in and out of the light. I watched so long that I must have fallen asleep at some point; it was such a mesmerizing sight.

Plus, we'd just had a pretty big day, given what had happened to us up on that mountain.

I felt a gentle nudge. "Suzanne, let's go upstairs. It's time for bed."

"I wasn't asleep," I protested, though it was clear to both of us that I was lying.

"I know, but we'll both be more comfortable up in our room. Besides, I can barely stay awake myself."

"Liar," I said with a grin. "The truth is that I am pretty beat."

"You have good reason to be," he said.

"Are you saying that you're really not tired?" I asked him.

"I would never say that. The truth is that I doubt I'll have any trouble nodding off tonight myself," he admitted.

"Well, if *you* need to get to bed early, then it's okay with me that we go back up to our room," I said as I stifled a yawn. I didn't care what the clock said.

I was tired, stiff, and more than a little sore, and I for one was ready to get some sleep.

Chapter 20

WHETHER IT WAS FROM the excitement of the day or just my normal routine of getting up in the middle of the night, I woke up abruptly and completely at 2:30 am. Jake stirred as I got out of bed, but he didn't wake up, which was a relief. Most nights when I woke up when I wasn't scheduled to be at the donut shop, I could trick myself into going back to sleep, but nothing worked this time.

I got dressed quietly and then wrote Jake a note in the light from my phone.

"Couldn't sleep. Going to the lobby to enjoy the fire! Love you, S."

I put the note on the dresser, and remembered to get my key as well. If I got drowsy sitting in front of the fireplace, I wanted to be able to come back to bed without waking my husband up.

I wasn't really all that surprised that no one else was in the lobby, not even someone on the desk. I had to figure that Jimmy Garrett's clerk was a no-show again, probably using the still-falling snow outside as an excuse, and that the innkeeper had probably had to collapse somewhere simply from lack of sleep and exhaustion. I didn't envy him the task ahead of him, even though at least he now knew that there wasn't going to be any competition for the Overlook, at least not in the near future, at any rate.

The fire in the hearth was beginning to die down a bit, so I took the poker and moved the coals around before adding a few of the nearby logs to the blaze. I nearly threw one of the short and skinny pieces of oak into the fire, but I finally decided to keep it out and add it later. Once the fire was going again in earnest, I watched the flames leap and dance while it continued to snow outside. Evidently Jimmy Garrett had forgotten to turn the outside lights off when he'd gone to bed, which was something I was thankful for at the moment.

I was perfectly content sitting on the couch and taking it all in when I suddenly realized that I was hungry. The only problem was that the food was in the kitchen, and I couldn't imagine that it wouldn't be locked at this time of night.

But maybe, just maybe, Jimmy had forgotten to lock it just as he'd neglected to turn off the floodlights.

With the log still in my hand, I walked in silence down the hallway into the dining room, and then toward the kitchen.

The door was locked solidly, and unless I was willing to break in to get a snack, I was going to have to wait until morning to get anything to eat.

I headed back toward the lobby when I walked past the photograph again that had set us off on our wild goose chase earlier. I couldn't make out the fine details of the image in the weakened light, but the signpost was unmistakably the same one Jake and I had explored all too thoroughly earlier in the day.

I pulled my phone out and read the message Tommy Malone had left for his sister, never knowing that she'd be dead before she'd had a chance to read it.

"Had to move the cursed thing again. COPS on my tail. UNDER DR101."

If that note hadn't been a clue to the whereabouts of the Star, then what could it have meant? Was it possible that it was some kind of secret code the brother and sister had used as kids? The DR1 had seemed so promising, too. Was there any *other* possible explanations as to what it might mean? No, it had to be the trail sign! Then what did the zero and the one mean, or the word 'Under' for that matter? It just didn't make sense.

Or did it?

I stared at the photo a full ten seconds more, and then I had a theory that was too crazy to even believe possible. There was no way it could be true, but I was certainly in the right place to check it out.

I tried to pull the photo off the wall, but it had been secured in place with screws that looked to be decades old. Clearly nobody had moved that photo in a very long time.

Maybe even since Tommy Gun Malone had hidden the Southern Shooting Star behind it.

I dropped the stick in my hands as I searched for something I could use to remove the old-fashioned slotted screws, and I started questioning my own sanity. Was I that far around the bend with my search for treasure that I was inventing solutions now? At least there was no one there to see me in my folly. I finally found a letter opener behind the desk that might work. As I labored at releasing the screws, I thought about the note again.

The word "under" may have been quite literal, meaning 'behind.' The DR1 was either the actual one-mile marker on the Devil's Ridge Loop Trail, or it signified the image I was looking at as I worked. What about the zero and the one, though?

What if that wasn't it, though? Maybe Momma had been right after all.

It could be a capital O and a capital I.

Overlook Inn.

He might just have been leading his sister there all along, only I'd been too blind to see it for what it was. There was nothing subtle about it, especially since Jimmy Garrett himself had told us earlier that Tommy Gun had stayed at the Overlook just before he was captured.

If only I was right.

The letter opener snapped as I was working on the second screw.

I had to face it. It was useless as a screwdriver. I shoved it into my pocket and went off in search of something else that might work instead.

I was about to give up when I decided to take a look around the lobby. Maybe something had fallen between the cushions that I could use.

Someone's penknife must have slipped out of their pocket.

There wasn't a screwdriver on it, but the blade itself might work. I could always replace the knife if I damaged it.

I finally got the second screw loose, and then I worked it slowly out by hand.

There was indeed a hollow opening behind the photograph, but once more, I came up empty.

If something had been there at one time, it was clearly gone now.

Chapter 21

I WAS ABOUT TO PUT the photograph back up, feeling foolish as I grabbed it from where I'd leaned it against the wall, when I remembered that the hole in the brick wall had appeared to be empty upon first look, too. Setting the photo back down, I took out my cell phone and tried to light the empty space inside of the cavity.

I couldn't see a thing, though, because of the angle.

Taking a deep breath, I shoved my hand into the opening and started feeling around.

I was almost ready to give up when my fingertips brushed against something soft.

I nearly screamed then, thinking it might be a rat, but then I realized that it wasn't moving. Besides, when I checked it out further, I knew that it had to be an old shirt, not a dead rodent's body.

Reaching in, cutting my arm slightly on the exposed wooden lath, I finally managed to pull whatever it was out of the wall.

It took my breath away, plain and simple. The gold shone as though it had just been cast, and the jewels that made up the tail of the shooting star were utterly amazing. They glimmered and danced in the light coming from the fireplace, and I knew beyond a shadow of a doubt that I was holding the Southern Shooting Star, famed for over a hundred years and lost for decades, in my hands.

I was so enthralled by the sight that I almost didn't hear the voice behind me.

"I can't believe you actually found it," Jimmy Garrett, the innkeeper, said.

As I turned around to show him my prize, I saw that his hands weren't empty, either.

He had a gun, and it was currently being aimed straight at my heart.

Chapter 22

"WHAT ARE YOU DOING, Jimmy?" I asked him. "You don't need that gun. There's nobody here but the two of us."

He looked wildly around the lobby and then the hallway. "Where's your husband?"

What I should have said was that he was in the kitchen so I could distract him long enough to make my move. What I said instead was, "He's still asleep upstairs," only realizing my mistake after the words had already left my lips.

"That's too bad for you," Jimmy said. "Hand it over, Suzanne. After all, it's rightfully mine, anyway."

"How do you figure that?" I asked him, not willing to give up the one advantage I had at the moment.

"I own the inn, and everything in it," he said. "It just makes sense."

"If you really believed that, you wouldn't be holding a gun on me, Jimmy," I argued.

"Perhaps there is some gray area," he conceded, "but we both know if lawyers get involved, they will be the *only* ones who win."

"How about this?" I asked, thinking as quickly as I could on my feet. "Why don't I hand it over to you right now, and then I promise to forget that I ever saw it. You can 'find' it again yourself after we're gone and collect the reward, or you can keep it all for yourself, and nobody will be the wiser."

The strapped innkeeper appeared to consider my offer, but then he shook his head. "I'm truly sorry, Suzanne, but I can't let there be any doubt that the Star is mine," he said. "What happens if you change your mind later? You could make things pretty uncomfortable for me. No, this way is cleaner."

"So, you're telling me that you're going to shoot me in cold blood for this piece of metal and stone in order to make sure I keep my mouth shut? My husband is sleeping one floor up. Do you honestly believe that he won't come running the second he hears a shot and realizes that I'm missing? You're not thinking straight, Jimmy."

"You're right," the innkeeper said. "Take out your phone and call him. Tell him you need him downstairs immediately, even that you found something, but if you say one word more, or even deviate one syllable from what I just told you to say, you're going to die instantly. I'll take my chances with your husband, but it won't matter to you, because you'll already be dead."

"If you think I'm going to lure my husband down here so you can kill him, too, you're sadly mistaken," I said. "What are you going to do, kill every guest on the property? That's going to look kind of suspicious, don't you think?"

"Stop talking and do as I say," he ordered. I could see his finger tighten on the trigger in the dim light coming from the other room. My eyes must have been getting used to the lower levels of light.

I pulled out my cell phone while withdrawing the letter opener at the same time.

Pretending to dial my husband's number, I said everything into thin air that Jimmy Garrett had told me to say.

It would have worked, too, if he hadn't made one more demand. "Let me have your phone now."

"Why?"

"I want to be sure you made the call," he answered.

I shrugged as I started to hand it to him. "Suit yourself."

I thought about dropping it, but I had something better in mind. As he reached for my cell phone, I lashed out with the letter opener.

I'd meant to stab him in the chest, but he deflected it automatically with his gun hand.

Instead of killing him, I managed to just make him angry, but there was some good news, too.

The sharp broken end of the letter opener drew blood.

He roared in pain, and I knew in an instant that there was one of two things I could do.

I could attack and try to wrestle the gun from him, maybe even using the Star as a club, or I could run.

He was too far away, I could see that in an instant, and by the time I got to him, I'd be dead.

So I ran.

Chapter 23

HE ACTUALLY SHOT AT me, something I never would have figured would actually happen. I had a hunch that his animal instincts were taking over now. He'd been wounded, and he wanted revenge.

And the Southern Shooting Star.

I could hear the bullet ricocheting off the wall as I ducked out the front door and into the snow.

Jimmy would be able to find me easily enough if I slowed down, so despite the pounding snow, the freezing cold, and the slick conditions, I ran as fast as I could into the night.

There were trees near the Overlook, and I headed for those, hoping to lose him there.

I might have made it, too, if those blasted floodlights hadn't been on.

They lit up the landscape as though it were high noon!

I made it to one of the trees just as a fresh bullet zinged its bark.

I knew that the next shot would be the last he'd have to fire.

It wasn't until then that I even realized that I still had the artifact in my grip. I had been unconsciously gripping it as though it were some kind of talisman against evil.

Instead, it had awakened the evil in a man I had considered basically good before he'd seen the gold and the jewels in my hand.

"Do you want this? Is this what you're after?" I asked as I waved it in the air. "Then go get it," I said as I heaved it as far as I could over the edge of the embankment toward the precipice below.

He screamed again as he watched it disappear into the night sky, but his protest didn't sound human this time.

Clearly without even hesitating, Jimmy Garrett went off the side of the cliff in search of his treasure, forgetting all about me, the gun in his hands, or the chance that he wouldn't survive the fall to the rocks below.

Chapter 24

"IS HE DEAD?" I ASKED Jake woodenly as he brought me another cup of hot chocolate. I knew without asking that the gunshot had woken him, just as I'd predicted, but Jimmy hadn't listened. Jake must have gotten outside just in time to see the inn's owner take his plunge. He'd rushed to protect me from the greedy potential killer, but he'd been too late to save the innkeeper. We'd stared down through the snow together on the edge of the precipice, but we couldn't see the body.

For all I knew, Jimmy could have survived the fall and grabbed the Star, and was even now making his escape.

I doubted it, but it was possible.

After the deputy sheriff arrived, he'd taken a search party down the hillside to see what had really happened to Jimmy Garrett.

"I haven't heard anything yet," Jake said as he sipped some of his own cocoa. "I can't believe you were the one to find that thing after all these years."

"And I'm also the person who almost got killed *twice* in less than twenty-four hours, too," I said. "I don't care if he got away. At this point, I'm just glad it's nothing I have to worry about anymore."

Jake didn't answer, and we sat there in silence until Deputy Alexander came in a few minutes later.

"No worries, folks. We got him," he said as he stamped the snow off his boots.

"Was he dead when you found him?" I asked again.

"No, but he messed up his leg pretty bad. The boys are carrying him out on a stretcher even as we speak."

"Did you find the Star?" Jake asked. "Suzanne is the one who found it before Jimmy got it."

Alexander grinned. "I've got it, all right, but it took us forever to pry it out of his hands." He pulled it out of his jacket and handed it to me. "I guess this is yours, at least until you can turn it over to the insurance people. We'll need it for evidence for the trial, but there's no reason you shouldn't spend at least a little time with it now."

"I don't want it," I said, remembering what had happened directly because of it.

"I'll take it," Jake said. To his credit, he barely looked at it.

"Like I said, I'll need it back when I leave. It's pretty though, isn't it?" he asked.

"I suppose so," Jake said.

I didn't even bother answering.

"Oh, by the way, you don't have to worry about Duncan and Henry anymore."

"Did you catch them, Deputy?" Jake asked.

"No, but a tree took care of that for us. Duncan had to be going seventy when his SUV slipped off the road and hit an oak head-on."

"They both died, didn't they?" I asked, feeling numb inside. How much death was going to be associated with that relic? Was it possible that it was actually cursed? More likely, the curse was the human condition of greed that yearned to possess it, even beyond reason.

"Duncan didn't make it, but Henry just got a few broken ribs and a cut over one eye. He had his seat belt on, but Duncan wasn't as smart. Anyway, I thought you should know."

"Thanks," I said. "What's going to happen to Jimmy Garrett?"

"First he's going to the hospital, and then he's going to jail," the deputy said. "I never would have thought Jimmy was capable of acting the way he did."

"You just never know, do you?" Jake asked.

"I do, and I don't like one single bit of it." I turned to my husband. "I don't care what it's worth. I meant what I said. I don't want it anywhere near us."

Jake rubbed my shoulder. "I understand. How about if we compromise? Let's give the Star back to the deputy, and once the trial is over, he can hand it directly over to the insurance company himself. Is that okay with you? Suzanne, the reward is yours. After all, you're the one who found it, and like you said, you almost died because of it not once but twice today, and most of all, you're the one who deserves the credit."

"No, I'm sorry, but it's not going to happen that way," I protested. "We'll all take credit for it, with Phillip taking the most. After all, if it hadn't been for him, I never would have found it." Somehow that seemed like a fit and proper solution to the dilemma.

And best of all, it meant that I never had to see the Southern Shooting Star again in my life.

Alexander took possession of it, and then he asked, "Are you folks going to be all right?"

"We are now," I said, suddenly feeling better now that the Southern Shooting Star was out of our lives.

I didn't need the gold, the jewels, or even the money for the reward it would surely bring us.

I already *had* everything I needed: a family that loved me, my health, and a purpose in life.

There might be nobler causes in the world than making donuts for the masses, but none were cut out for me.

Unlike others who had been searching for the Star along with the four of us, I'd found my way in the world, and no amount of wealth could ever change that.

RECIPES

Cranberry Chocolate Donut Drops

I go through phases where I can't get enough cranberries in my treats, and I created this recipe during one of those times. It's one of the easiest donuts I've ever made and also one of my favorites. Sometimes I feel like concocting an intricate recipe with multiple risings and complicated ingredient lists, and sometimes I just want something tasty, quick, and easy to make. I know I probably shouldn't admit that, but it's true nonetheless.

The base of this recipe is a simple 7-ounce biscuit mix, but adding the cranberries and the bittersweet chocolate chips takes it to a whole new level. Top the finished fried treats with powdered sugar, chocolate drizzle, or eat plain. Any way you serve these, they'll be a hit.

Ingredients

1 packet (7 oz.) biscuit mix (plain, or use your imagination!)

1/2 cup whole or 2% milk

2 tablespoons granulated sugar

1/3 cup dried cranberries (raisins will work as well)

2 tablespoons bittersweet chocolate chips

Directions

Heat enough canola oil to cover your donuts as they are frying to 360 degrees F.

While you're waiting for the oil to hit the proper temperature, take a medium bowl and add the biscuit mix, milk, and sugar, stirring thoroughly but not too much. Stop when the biscuit mix is almost entirely incorporated into the slurry. Next, add cranberries and chocolate chips and mix until combined.

When the oil is ready, drop pieces of dough using two tablespoons or a cookie scoop in. Fry for 3 to 4 minutes, flipping once halfway through.

Drain on paper towels then coat while still warm and enjoy!

Yields 10 to 12 donut drops.

A New Style Donut for Everyone

I've heard all of the fuss about a cronutty recipe sweeping the country, so I thought I'd try my hand at making one as well. I've never had one of the originals, but if they are anything like this one, prepare yourself for a decadent treat. This process is a bit convoluted and is not for the faint of heart, but if you have some time and want to take a swing at it, be my guest! Be prepared to spend some time making these, though. Unlike the recipe above, these are neither simple nor quick, but they are delicious!

Ingredients

1/2 teaspoon Rapid Rise yeast

1/4 cup water, warm

2 eggs, beaten

1/2 cup whole or 2% milk

8 tablespoons unsalted butter, melted, divided into three equal portions

3 tablespoons granulated white sugar

1 teaspoon vanilla extract

1/2 teaspoon nutmeg

1/2 teaspoon cinnamon

1/4 teaspoon salt

3 to 4 cups regular all-purpose flour (bleached or unbleached)

Glaze

1 cup confectioner's sugar

1/2 teaspoon vanilla extract

1 to 2 tablespoons buttermilk, as needed (whole, 2%, or 1% will do fine as a substitute)

Oil for Frying

Canola or peanut oil, about 1 quart

Directions

In a stand mixer, combine warm water with yeast and wait 5 minutes for it to activate.

Next, mix in beaten eggs, milk, 1/3 of the butter, sugar, vanilla extract, nutmeg, cinnamon, and salt. Mix on low for 1 minute.

Next, add 1 1/2 cups of flour, mixing until it's incorporated, and then keep adding a cup at a time.

Next, I change from a whisk to a dough hook attachment and continue until it forms a smooth and consistent ball. Remove from the mixer and wrap in plastic wrap before refrigerating 1/2 hour.

After 30 minutes are up, take out the ball and roll out on a lightly dusted surface until it is approximately 1/4 inch thick. Spread out the second third of your reserved butter in the middle of the flattened dough, and then fold into thirds. Spread the last 1/3 of your butter and repeat, bringing it down to 1/4 inch thick again. Lightly grease a pan and place your dough on it, cover it with plastic wrap, and put back into the fridge for another 30 minutes.

After the 30 minutes are up, remove the dough and turn out onto a lightly floured surface again. Gently pat it out until it forms a sheet 8 by 12 inches. It should be approximately 1/4 inch thick now. Fold the dough into thirds again, then cover in wrap and refrigerate for 2 1/2 to 3 hours.

Finally, roll out the dough again on a lightly floured surface to approximately 1/4 inch thick, and then, using your donut cutter, cut out donuts and place them on a greased cookie sheet. Let them rise for an hour, and then drop them into Canola oil heated to 360 degrees F.

Fry the donut rounds and holes for 2 minutes per side, flipping over halfway through. The donuts should puff up as they cook.

Drain them on a wire rack, and then drizzle with glaze or dust with confectioner's sugar.

Yields 10 to 12 donuts and matching holes

Hot Chocolate Donut Delights

I love hot chocolate almost as much as Suzanne and her family do, so when I had a yen for some of that delicious beverage in donut form, I got cracking on a new recipe. Suzanne's turned out better than mine did, but hey, she's a professional donut maker, while I'm just someone who records her exploits and recipes for the world. If you're in a hot chocolaty mood, give these a try.

Ingredients

Dry

1 cup all-purpose flour (unbleached or bleached are both fine)

1/2 cup hot chocolate mix (see my recipe below, or use a store-bought powder)

1 teaspoon baking powder

1/4 teaspoon nutmeg

1/4 teaspoon cinnamon

1/4 teaspoon baking soda

1/8 teaspoon salt

Wet

1 egg, beaten

1/2 cup chocolate milk (2% or whole preferred)

3 tablespoons unsalted butter, melted

1/2 cup granulated sugar

1 teaspoon vanilla extract

Directions

Preheat your oven to 350 degrees F.

While you're waiting for the oven to reach its desired temperature, sift together in a large bowl the flour, hot chocolate mix, baking powder, nutmeg, cinnamon, baking soda, and salt.

In a separate bowl, combine beaten egg, chocolate milk, butter, sugar, and vanilla.

Slowly add this wet mix to the dry, stirring until it's incorporated.

Bake for 10 to 12 minutes in cupcake trays or donut molds.

Remove from the oven and transfer to a cooling rack when an inserted toothpick comes out clean, or with a few crumbs at most.

For an added bonus, these can be dusted with cocoa powder, iced with chocolate glaze, or eaten just as they are, fresh out of the oven.

Makes 10 to 12 donuts.

The Very Best Hot Chocolate I've Ever Had

Here's a hot chocolate mix that my family and I created years ago in our search for the perfect hot cocoa. We love this particular blend, but feel free to experiment with a mix that's all your own. After all, that's part of the fun of working together in the kitchen!

Ingredients

2 cups powdered milk

3/4 cup granulated sugar

1/2 cup nondairy creamer, powdered

1/2 cup Hershey's Cocoa, natural unsweetened powder

1/2 cup Special Dark Hershey's Cocoa, Dutch Processed powder

2 dashes of salt

3/4 cup hot milk (whole or 2%) with 1/4 to 1/3 cup dry mix added and thoroughly stirred in.

Directions

In a large bowl, combine powdered milk, granulated sugar, nondairy creamer powder, unsweetened cocoa powder, Dutch Processed cocoa powder, and salt.

Sift together, and then store in an airtight container until you are ready to use it. Add to heated milk, stir thoroughly, and enjoy!

I've never counted how many cups this recipe actually makes, since we all use different amounts of the blend in our hot chocolate, but it's enough to usually get three of us through a cold month!

If you enjoy Jessica Beck Mysteries and you would like to be notified when the next book is being released, please visit our website at jessicabeckmysteries.net for valuable information about Jessica's books, and sign up for her new-releases-only mail blast.

Your email address will not be shared, sold, bartered, traded, broadcast, or disclosed in any way. There will be no spam from us, just a friendly reminder when the latest book is being released, and of course, you can drop out at any time.

Other Books by Jessica Beck

The Donut Mysteries
Glazed Murder
Fatally Frosted
Sinister Sprinkles
Evil Éclairs
Tragic Toppings
Killer Crullers
Drop Dead Chocolate
Powdered Peril
Illegally Iced
Deadly Donuts
Assault and Batter
Sweet Suspects
Deep Fried Homicide
Custard Crime
Lemon Larceny
Bad Bites
Old Fashioned Crooks
Dangerous Dough
Troubled Treats
Sugar Coated Sins
Criminal Crumbs
Vanilla Vices
Raspberry Revenge
Fugitive Filling
Devil's Food Defense
Pumpkin Pleas
Floured Felonies
Mixed Malice

Tasty Trials
Baked Books
Cranberry Crimes
Boston Cream Bribes
Cherry Filled Charges
Scary Sweets
Cocoa Crush
Pastry Penalties
Apple Stuffed Alibies
Perjury Proof
Caramel Canvas
Dark Drizzles
Counterfeit Confections
Measured Mayhem
Blended Bribes
Sifted Sentences
Dusted Discoveries

The Classic Diner Mysteries
A Chili Death
A Deadly Beef
A Killer Cake
A Baked Ham
A Bad Egg
A Real Pickle
A Burned Biscuit
The Ghost Cat Cozy Mysteries
Ghost Cat: Midnight Paws
Ghost Cat 2: Bid for Midnight
The Cast Iron Cooking Mysteries
Cast Iron Will

Cast Iron Conviction
Cast Iron Alibi
Cast Iron Motive
Cast Iron Suspicion
Nonfiction
The Donut Mysteries Cookbook

Made in the USA
Monee, IL
07 February 2020

21452704R00095